ZAVEN

A House of Ausher Novella

EMBER DRAKE

CAN THE COLD
HEART OF DEATH
LEARN TO LOVE?

ZAVEN

A House of Ausher Novella

EMBER DRAKE

First paperback edition August 2025

Book cover design by Ember Drake on BookBrush.com and Canva.com

ISBN 979-8-9902478-4-0 (paperback)

Content/Trigger Warning

Warnings for Zaven contain intense and potentially upsetting themes, including:

- ❖ Death by execution
- ❖ Explicit sexual content

CHAPTER 1

Nestled between the winding embrace of slow-moving rivers and the vast, reflective surface of an old lake, the village was a hushed sanctuary, cradled by nature's abundance. Thick woods pressed in from the outskirts, their towering oaks forming a protective boundary, casting elongated shadows across the dirt paths that weaved between timber-framed homes with thatched roofs. Smoke curled lazily from stone chimneys; a sign of hearty meals being prepared in simple but sturdy hearths.

At the first light of dawn, the mist rose from the lake like ghostly fingers, drifting across the water in tendrils before dissipating under the first golden rays of sunlight. Fishermen pushed their worn wooden boats into the shallows, their nets heavy with expectation. The rivers, their waters rich with silver-scaled fish, provided both food and a silent connection to the outside world. Though few travelers ventured that far. The air was thick with the scent of damp earth, moss, and wild herbs, carried on a perpetual breeze that whispered secrets between reeds.

In the village square—little more than a clearing ringed by wooden stalls—the blacksmith hammered away at his forge, the rhythmic clang echoing through the trees. A modest chapel stood at the highest point, its weather-worn bell a lonely voice calling the villagers to worship or warning of approaching storms. The festivals were unpretentious, but lively. The villagers gathered to celebrate the harvest with rustic music, dancing, and feasts laid out on wooden tables beneath glittering lanterns.

Among the fields, neat patches of barley, rye, and oats were cultivated, essential for bread, porridge, and ale—staples of survival. Closer to the homes, vegetable gardens flourished with clusters of turnips, cabbages, and beans, their roots thick with earth, pulled fresh for evening meals. Fragrant herbs—thyme, sage, and rosemary—spilled over wooden planters near stone hearths, drying in bundles for cooking and medicine.

Orchards lay just beyond the village's edges, their trees weighed down with apples, pears, and plums, their blossoms drifting on the breeze in spring. Grapevines crept along wooden trellises, nurtured by skilled hands for rudimentary winemaking. The lake's edge served another role, where small rice paddies shimmered in the shallows, their stalks half-submerged, soaking in the nutrients.

When the harvest season arrived, the village hummed with activity. Bundles of grain stacked high, barrels of fruit preserved, and root vegetables stored carefully for the colder months. Those crops were more than mere sustenance. They were woven into the villagers' way of life, dictating feasts, trade, and survival in their quiet sanctuary.

Life was slow, deliberate—each season shaping the village's existence. The lake, the rivers, the endless forest beyond—they formed both refuge and barrier, isolating the village from the grand upheavals of the world beyond its borders.

Yet the air pulsed with change, a harbinger howling just beyond the veil.

CHAPTER 2

Drowned souls never struggled once they reached the celestial tides. Their bodies—or rather, their remnants—floated like pale fragments of forgotten prayers. They did not wail, did not plead. Their final moments, the gasping, the clawing desperation—were long gone. They were calm now. Silent. That was how they should be.

The celestial tides ebbed and flowed in silence, carrying the echoes of the drowned to their final rest. Zaven watched without emotion, perched at the edge of the silver shores where drowned souls rose from the depths like mist. His duty was simple. Escort them to their eternity, neither mourning their fate nor marveling at the lives they once lived.

Ozmir, Zaven's twin and keeper of the drowned souls, stood beside him that day, arms crossed and visage sharp with frustration. He did not see things as Zaven saw them.

"You could at least pretend to care," Ozmir snapped, his voice unsettling the quiet sea beneath them. "These souls suffered. They grasped at the last breath of life, begging for salvation. And you—" He gestured at Zaven's detached stare. "You act as if they're nothing more than waves breaking against the shore."

Zaven let out a puff of air, unfazed. "They are what they are. Drowned souls. They're here now, and they'll be elsewhere soon. What difference does it make how I feel about it?"

Zaven did not look at him. The souls drifted past him, moving toward their eternity. And he walked as he always did, beside them, but never truly with them.

"They suffered, Zaven," Ozmir spoke, watching the latest arrival with something that nearly resembled grief, before jogging to catch up with his brother. "Their last moments were filled with terror. And you treat them as if they are nothing. As if they were never real at all."

"What would you have me do?" Zaven asked, his voice even as the tide beneath them. "Weep for every soul that touches the shore? Would that undo their drowning? Would that change the way the water took them?"

Ozmir made a sound, something harsh and exasperated. Zaven knew what he wanted. He wanted something he could not give—attachment, sorrow, weight. The souls belonged to the water now, and he would not anchor himself to them.

They passed through the tides, and he remained as he was. Unmoved. Unchanging. But Ozmir had a look that knew that somewhere beneath Zaven's cool indifference, there was something restless. Something in Zaven flickered, if only for an instant, before sinking beneath the tide again.

The celestial tides whispered, endless and unchanging, but Ozmir's voice grated against the tranquility like a jagged stone.

"You're impossible," he huffed, stepping into Zaven's path. "How can you stand there surrounded by death and feel nothing?"

Zaven exhaled slowly. He had long since stopped looking at his brother when he spoke like that. His frustration was familiar. A ceaseless tide that crashed over Zaven again and again but never eroded his patience. Or at least, that was what he told himself. His twin was a bleeding heart.

"It is not my place to feel," he replied, his voice still steady. "I escort them to you. That is all."

Ozmir scoffed. "Cold. Detached. Empty." He shook his head, his golden hair catching the dim glow of the drifting souls. "What a fine existence you've made for yourself."

Zaven stopped walking.

The tides continued their quiet procession, but Zaven was still. Still enough that Ozmir finally took notice, finally paused. The weight of his words, of his endless prodding, grated against something in Zaven he did not care to name.

"You waste words, brother," he said, turning to him fully now. "Nagging will not shape me into the thing you want. I do what is required. That is enough. You need to let go of your attachment to them. It won't serve you well."

Ozmir's mouth gaped open, another rebuke forming, but Zaven raised his hand, silencing him. His patience was not infinite. It had frayed enough.

"Go, tend to your echoes," he said, cool and final. "And let me tend to mine."

For a moment, only the waves spoke. Ozmir watched his brother, his expression torn between frustration and something deeper. Then, with a sharp outlet of air, he turned on his heel and vanished into the ether.

Zaven resumed his walk.

"Well, that was a bit cold," muttered a soul.

"Be silent," Zaven grumbled in reply.

The souls continued their procession. The tides whispered on. And for now, at least, the silence was his.

Chapter 3

Each morning, just as the golden light spilled through the space between the worn curtains, she rose. The scent of dried herbs filled her cottage, mingling with the crisp air drifting through the open window. Airlia stretched and yawned, sluggishly blinking the sleep from her still tired eyes. Her mass of fiery-red hair stuck out in all directions as she ran her hands through it. Putting on her slippers, she went to check on her father in the next room. His frail form rested quietly beneath layers of blankets, his breath steady but weak. She murmured to him softly, a ritual of comfort, before setting out.

The morning was her favorite time, and the forest that surrounded her home was her sanctuary. The soft rustle of leaves, the crisp air that carried the scent of earth and dew—it was all hers. Basket in hand, she moved through the undergrowth with practiced ease, collecting leaves, roots, and blossoms, each one selected with the precision of a healer's touch.

As she gathered herbs, her fingers traced each leaf carefully, a silent gratitude whispered to nature for its endless gifts. She thought of her father, of how his hands once moved with the same precision and care when teaching her the art of healing. A pang of sorrow stirred, but she quickly tucked it away. There was no room for sadness, not when there was work to be done.

The villagers knew where to find her; kneeling by the river, humming softly as she crushed ingredients into pastes and powders. Her cheeks were flushed with heat as she toiled, sweat beading across her brow. Her hands were covered with dirt, and they ached. The river hummed softly as Airlia knelt by the bank, dipping her hands into the cool water to soothe them. The morning sun glinted against the surface, sending ripples of light dancing across her fingers. She closed her eyes for a brief moment, allowing the serenity to settle into her bones.

"You always come here alone," came a familiar voice drifting from behind her.

He did not startle her—she had long since learned the weight of his presence. Turning just a hair, she found him standing a few feet away, his arms crossed, watching her with that quiet intensity he always carried. He was never forceful, never demanding, but he was always there, waiting.

"And yet, you always find me," she replied, brushing a stray red lock of hair from her face.

Eldrin was not like her other suitors who brought flowers or poetry, hoping for a fleeting glance from Airlia. He had spent years trying to understand her—not just her beauty, but the weight she carried. A skilled hunter and tracker, he moved through the forest as effortlessly as the wind, always returning with offerings. Rare herbs she might need, pelts to keep her father warm, quiet gestures of devotion rather than grand declarations of love.

He stepped closer, crouching beside her, resting his forearms against his knees. "I see you carrying the weight of the village on your shoulders, Airlia. Do you ever rest?"

She let out air gradually, staring at the water. "Healing is not something that stops. If I do, someone suffers."

He studied her in silence, then reached into the pouch at his side, pulling out a small bundle wrapped in cloth. He handed it to her. "Lavender. You need to sleep."

Airlia hesitated, her fingers brushing against the fabric. She knew Eldrin—knew that this was how he spoke, through gestures rather than words. She knew this was not another attempt to win her affections, but something simpler. Genuine care.

But Airlia remained unmoved. Though she appreciated his kindness, she never encouraged his affections. Still, Eldrin did not give up. She assumed he thought her simply too burdened to consider love, that one day, she might open her heart to him. And so, he lingered—watching from the edges, waiting for a moment when she might need him.

She accepted the flowers, the slightest smile touching her lips. "Thank you."

For a moment, neither of them spoke. The river continued its steady song; the wind shifting through the trees. Eldrin watched her, as he always did—never expectant, never impatient. Just present.

And perhaps, Airlia thought, she did not mind it.

He stood, stretching as he did so. "Take care, Airlia. You're no good to your father if you get sick." With that, he disappeared into the woods.

By midday, she was back in the village, deep in her work—grinding roots, binding wounds, soothing fevered brows. She moved between cottages, offering remedies and easing the pain of those that could not make it to her healing hut. Some approached her shyly, offering her tokens of gratitude—a fresh loaf of bread, a woven ribbon, a whispered blessing. She never asked for payment, yet the village found a way to give.

She listened to their stories as she worked; the villagers confiding their worries and joys. Naturally, she smiled and nodded to reassure them. In those moments, she felt most alive, as though the very act of healing wove her into the fabric of something greater than herself.

Returning home in the afternoon, she paused in front of the doorway. Her father's frail frame reminded her that time was slipping away, no matter how fiercely she fought against it. She looked down at her hands; they were stained with earth and tinctures. He opened the door, smiling as brightly as he could at her.

"Welcome home, my dear," he said, his voice gravelly with age. He took hold of her hands, making a feeble attempt to dust them off. "You work too hard. Come inside and rest."

She allowed him to guide her into their home, hoping she hid her melancholy about his poor condition well. Once inside, she brewed tea for her father while he fussed gently for her to rest and not trouble herself. While he grumbled, she told him of the day's events as she brushed back his thinning hair with care.

"Eldrin is a fine young man, Airlia. He would make a good husband for you," he spoke, sipping his tea.

Airlia gave her father a knowing look. "He is, and he would be. For someone else. I have all I need with my work, and I have you to care for."

"But I won't be around forever, dear one."

"Shush, now. Just let me do what I can while you're still here," she fussed lightly, taking his empty cup to the small kitchen. But she knew he was right. He did not have much time left in this world.

Once she put her father down for the night, she readied herself for bed. As dusk painted the sky in hues of deep violet and fiery red—so much like her own hair—she sat by the window, watching the world quiet around her. Yet her mind was restless. Was this all there was? Was there something beyond the village, beyond the life she had built? While she did not long for adventure, an unnamed yearning stirred deep within her. Tomorrow would come, and she would wake to the same routine, the same faces, the same duties. And yet, something felt different—like the wind was whispering of change.

CHAPTER 4

Whispering against the ruined shore, the tides curled over bones half-buried in the silt. The scent of salt and decay lingered, a slow-creeping thing that clung to the air. Zaven stood at the edge, his cloak heavy, stiff with salty water. He locked onto something that had been lost for a while—a trembling soul, still slick with the weight of its final breath.

Zaven's familiar, Lux, perched on a jagged rock, flicked his tail in irritation. "Must you scowl like that, Zaven? You terrify them more than the drowning did."

Nox, Lux's partner, and always dramatic, purred lazily nearby. "He's all grumbles and glarin'. It's unpleasant. The whole transition would go smoother if he learned a bit of bedside manner."

Zaven exhaled angrily, the sound rumbling through his chest like waves against the cliffs. He was used to this. Lux and Nox always had something to say, always found some flaw in how he did his work. The first hundred times, he had ignored them outright. The next hundred, he had grunted in vague acknowledgement. But now—now, their needling stuck in his ribs like fishhooks.

Not because they were wrong.

The soul before him quivered, wispy and fragile, not yet resigned to its fate. It should have passed into the depths with grace long ago. Acceptance. But no—fear clung to it, turning its edges jagged, restless. It feared *him*.

He clenched his jaw. "They're dead. There's no comfort left to give."

Lux rolled his golden eyes, his ink-black fur bristling faintly as he leapt from the rock and landed at Zaven's feet. "Oh, sure, because being led to eternity by you is such a treat." His tail flicked, sharp and impatient. "Maybe if you stopped looming, they wouldn't panic every time you reached for them."

Zaven stiffened, the weight of his presence pressing against the space around him like the pull of an undertow. What did they expect? Did they think he could whisper soothing words, trace gentle fingers through the remnants of their earthly forms, promise that the depths held something kinder than oblivion? He had seen thousands pass into his domain.

And it was always the same.

The flinching. The dread. The final, irreversible descent.

Nox groaned. "See? This is what we mean."

Zaven's glare was intense enough to cut through fog. "You do it then."

The familiars exchanged glances, then took a step back. Nox coughed, tail curling as she sat. "Well, ya are the god of drowned souls. Not much we can do about the whole 'menacing presence' thing."

Lux sighed, his tail flicking again, agitated. "Just—try not to make them feel like they're sinking all over again."

Zaven narrowed his eyes, but said nothing. The tide swelled against the shore, curling over bone and stone, and he reached once more for the soul. This time, though, it shivered, it did not pull away.

Baby steps, perhaps.

CHAPTER 5

The ethereal glow that once adorned Zaven's form had dimmed, leaving him as nothing more than a solitary figure beneath the mortal sky. The celestial realm felt distant—almost like a dream slipping through his fingers. In the mortal world, the air was different. It carried the scent of damp earth, the whisper of grass as the wind wove through it. The river reflected the sky in silvery ripples, mirroring the clouds as they drifted without purpose.

In the quiet refuge by the river's edge, he let the world breathe around him. Zaven sat beneath the shade of an ancient willow, his posture rigid, his gaze locked on the water, yet his mind was far away.

He had wandered down from the heavens to be alone, to reflect and understand. He had seen himself through countless souls, watched them plead, rejoice, crumble under the weight of their own existence. And yet, he had never truly understood them. Always distant. Always cold.

Then his gaze shifted.

Beyond the riverbank, she moved—light-footed, radiant. She knelt amid the wildflowers, her fingers brushing against the herbs with reverence. Golden light traced itself into the fiery locks of her hair, a cascade of warmth against the deep greens of her surroundings. She worked with quiet concentration, each movement filled with intention. A careful plucking of leaves, a soft hum in the air, as though she was speaking to the land itself.

She was unlike anything he had ever seen. Effortlessly resplendent yet deeply grounded in the pulse of life around her.

Zaven did not move.

Something unfamiliar stirred within him—an ache, perhaps, or a curiosity too keen to ignore. He had seen beauty before; the celestial halls brimmed with it, perfection crafted into every curve, every light-drenched corridor. But this was different. She was not divine, nor crafted with intention. She simply was—earthly, warm, real. A gentle breeze lifted the edge of her sleeves, carrying with it the scent of crushed lavender and thyme. And for the first time in his long existence, he found himself wondering—what would it be like to step forward? To speak? To be seen? But he remained in the shadows, silent, watching.

A spectator to something he did not yet understand.

Zaven remained cloaked in the shade of the willow, his presence unnoticed, his thoughts unraveling like threads pulled too tightly. He watched the red-haired woman as she moved with practiced grace, the hem of her simple dress brushing against the wild flora. As she continued to pick herbs, each gesture revealed a quiet intimacy with the earth. Her fingers brushed against the leaves, inspecting them with the discerning eye of someone who understood their worth beyond mere appearance. She gathered them gently, tucking each stem into the woven basket at her side, careful not to damage their fragile veins. There was a reverence in the way she worked—an unspoken dialogue between herself and the land, as though she knew its secrets, as if it trusted her in return.

Zaven had seen healers before, had witnessed their desperate attempts to mend the broken, to ease suffering that stretched beyond mortal hands. But none had moved as she did—without urgency or desperation. There was only calm, only certainty, only the soothing rhythm of work done with devotion.

A gust of wind stirred the meadow once more, sending ripples through the tall grass, carrying her scent toward him again. It was grounding, rich with life—so different from the hollow perfection of the celestial realm. There, scents were ethereal, never tied to anything tangible. But here? Here, the fragrance clung to the air, real and undeniable.

She reached for another bundle of herbs, pausing just briefly to brush her wrist against her forehead, smoothing away the sweat from the warmth of the morning sun. It was such a simple thing, yet Zaven found himself transfixed by it—this unconscious act, this small glimpse into her humanity.

He had never known fatigue, his heart did not beat, and he drew no breath. But watching her, he realized how little he understood of the world he had so often judged from afar.

And, for the first time, he wondered—if she turned, if she saw him, would she be afraid? Or would she recognize that, for all his cold indifference, something within him had begun to thaw?

Chapter 6

The celestial hall trembled with laughter—shrill, mocking, and cruel. Several gods lounged on their thrones of marble and gold, their voices weaving together in a chorus of ridicule.

"Ozmir the Gentle," mocked Vigita, a god of war, his plated gauntlet curling into a fist. "A deity who weeps for mortals, and clings to sentiment like a child to a broken toy."

A'kahli, goddess of storms, smirked. "Perhaps he should trade his divinity for a mortal heart. It would suit him better."

Their laughter grew, a roaring tide in the great hall, but Ozmir, the youngest among them, stood silent in the midst of it all—his silver robes pooling around him like moonlight, his expression calm but wounded.

Then, the laughter was cut like a string snapped mid-note.

A dark presence unfurled at the far end of the chamber.

Zaven. He had been listening, hoping his twin would stand up for himself, that he would not have to interfere again.

He was not loud. He did not need to be. His mere arrival sent a hush through the hall, as though the very air recognized the weight of his authority.

"You mistake mercy for weakness." His voice was measured, smooth as obsidian. "And in doing so, you reveal your own shallowness."

Vigita straightened, his amusement cooling into something darker. "We speak of balance, Zaven. A god should be mighty, feared."

"And yet, what is might without wisdom? Fear without love?" Zaven took a step forward, his midnight cloak sweeping over the polished floor. "Ozmir's heart is vast, and in that vastness, he is stronger than any of you who find pleasure in cruelty."

A'kahli narrowed her eyes. "You defend him as if he is incapable of standing on his own."

Zaven fixed his gaze onto Ozmir. The gentleness in his eyes was rare, fleeting, but undeniable. He had gotten into many altercations with his older siblings over his twin. Nothing had changed. But he had earned their respect and fear. He returned his attention to the gathering. "I defend him because I tire of watching small minds attempt to diminish something they don't understand."

The room paused. It was heavy and unyielding.

With a sharp exhalation, Vigita shook his head. "You waste breath on sentiment."

"And you waste yours on ignorance," Zaven countered. His tone was not heated—just final.

The hall remained silent long after, as the gods, one by one, found themselves without retort.

"Let's go, Ozzy," Zaven grumbled, turning to leave.

Ozmir stood there, stunned.

"Ozmir!" Zaven called when he noticed his brother was not behind him.

The celestial halls lay behind them, the echoes of laughter and argument fading into memory. Now, only the sky stretched before them—vast and unbroken, painted in hues of twilight. Ozmir stood on the edge of a marble terrace, his hands resting lightly on the railing. He exhaled softly, as if weary of everything.

Zaven approached, his footsteps nearly silent. For a long moment, he said nothing, simply studying the god beside him. Then—quietly—he spoke.

"They will not change," he murmured. "Not easily."

Ozmir let out a humorless chuckle, his silver robes rippling in the evening breeze. "No, they will not."

Silence settled between them—comfortable, not strained.

Then Ozmir turned his head, his countenance thoughtful. "You did not have to defend me."

Zaven tilted his head slightly. "I did."

Ozmir smiled, faint but genuine. "You always make things sound so absolute."

"Because they are." Zaven stepped forward, resting his arms against the railing beside his brother. He watched the flickering lights below, his expression unreadable. "They think kindness is weakness. But I know otherwise." He glanced toward Ozmir. "And so do you."

Ozmir studied him as if he were searching for something unspoken in the depths of Zaven's gaze. He found it—not pity, not obligation, but respect. A rare, unwavering thing. "You are strange, Zaven," he eventually said.

"And you are frustrating," Zaven replied, his tone as dry as the wind.

Ozmir chuckled. It was quiet, but real.

For now, the gods could keep their derision.

CHAPTER 7

The river was calm, its surface dappled with golden morning light. Airlia knelt among the reeds, fingers brushing against the delicate stems of wildflowers, the scent soft and soothing. She had been gathering herbs for nearly an hour, the basket beside her growing heavier with fragrant bundles.

A sudden shift in the wind sent a ripple across the water—a whisper, a warning. She turned her head just as her foot slipped on the moss-slick bank. There was no time to cry out. One moment, solid earth beneath her—the next, cold water swallowing her whole.

The current was stronger than it looked, a silent predator surging beneath the river's placid face. It caught her ankles first, yanking her off balance, then wrapped around her like coils of invisible rope, dragging her under. Her limbs flailed. Kicking, clawing, but every movement felt sluggish, energy sapped by the icy grip of panic and the river's relentless pull.

Her dress, once light and flowing, now clung to her like a drowning shroud, the sodden fabric wrapping around her legs, tangling her arms. Cold water surged into her nose and mouth as she gasped, coughing bubbles that streamed toward the dim, fractured light above. Her lungs screamed, each second stretching longer than the last. She tried to swim upward, but her body betrayed her. It was too lead-heavy and slow.

The sunlight danced just out of reach, a broken mosaic of gold on a ceiling that seemed impossibly far. Her ears filled with the roar of churning water and her own heartbeat, frantic and thudding like a drum. Darkness gathered at the edges of her vision, thick and clinging, like wet silk sliding over her skin. It whispered of surrender. Of letting go.

Then—something.

An unseen force. Arms, strong and deliberate, wrapped around her, guiding her upward. She barely registered the cold, the steadiness. Airlia broke the surface, gasping as her body seized, air strangled in her throat, her shivering as the river released her. She was no longer in the water, but it still owned her, wrapping cold fingers around her limbs, pressing phantom weight against her chest.

She coughed, the taste of river salt thick on her tongue, but the sensation that gripped her was not just fear. I was something deeper, something nameless.

A manifestation. A force.

Something had pulled her back from death, yet she could not grasp its shape. She barely comprehended the firm grip that placed her onto solid ground, the gentleness that lingered for a fraction of a second before vanishing like mist.

Again, she coughed, spitting water onto the dirt, blinking the blurriness from her eyes.

Eldrin's voice reached her like a distant echo, shaking her loose from the void.

"Airlia!" His hands steadied her shoulders. Warm, too human, too real. He was crouched beside her, his hand skimming over her to check for injuries. "What happened? You..." his eyes skimmed to the river, brows furrowing. "How did you get out?"

"I-I don't know." Her voice trembled, her fingers digging into the earth beneath her as though it might still slip from under her. "I was drowning, and then... someone pulled me out. But I didn't see..." She swallowed, turning toward the river, expecting what? A shadow, a handprint in the mud, proof that something had touched her?

But there was nothing.

Only the water. Still. Innocent. Lying.

"I don't know," she whispered, hugging her arms to herself.

Eldrin scanned the surroundings, then shook his head. "No one else is here."

Yet, she knew that was not true. She knew something had been there—something strong, something unseen. And though she was alive, she felt its lingering grip, like a breathless reminder that she had been claimed, if only for a moment.

CHAPTER 8

Far beyond them, hidden within the dense shade of trees, Zaven watched. He had not meant to intervene. He had told himself he would not. Gods were not permitted to directly interfere with a mortal's destiny. But when the river had turned cruel, when she had gone under, something in him refused to stay still.

Now, as she shivered beside another man, confusion etched into her features, he felt both satisfaction and regret battling within him.

She could not know. Not yet.

"Zaven Lareceun, you ought to be ashamed of yourself," came a familiar baritone.

Zaven sighed as he sat on the grass. He was dry. Water did not stick to him. As the god of drowned souls, he could manipulate any and every source of water. Including blood. "Not now, Lux."

"You know you're not allowed to—"

With a simple gesture of his hand, a tightly closed fist in the air, Lux had been felled. "I said not now." He did not bother to look at the body that fell with a soft thud behind him. It was not his intention to kill his familiar, but he was in no mood to be lectured. To see the woman he had been watching and admiring in the arms of another did not sit right with him. Something inside him, something he could not name, did not understand, burned for her.

Airlia. Her name was Airlia. The name suited her. She was ethereal with her fiery red hair, lustrous blue eyes, and creamy white skin. He wondered if she would accept someone like him, with his patches of scales in random places. His cold demeanor. His short temper.

Again, he sighed, then turned around to see Lux's twisted form on the ground, now stained with his blood. Zaven looked back to Airlia and the stranger at her side. He was helping her to her feet, steadying her when she stumbled. Then they left the riverside, his arms tight around her shoulders. Zaven frowned at that.

He wanted to punish the man for touching her. But he could not be seen. He was not ready. So, he returned his attention to his dead familiar. With a flourish of his hands, the grass around Lux's body was drained of its vibrant green color, turning brown and wilting. The trees closest to them did the same. Fingers, long and dark, moved sluggishly, grasping the earth beneath them. A long groan followed by a frustrated growl escaped Lux as he struggled to his feet.

The look he gave Zaven was deadly. Zaven offered an apologetic smile.

"Do you have any idea how much that hurts?" Lux growled. "You can't keep doing that! And what took you so long to bring me back?"

Zaven pointed over his shoulder. "Had to wait for the mortals to leave."

Lux looked to where Zaven was pointing. His eyes narrowed. "What if they hadn't left?" he asked, returning his gaze to Zaven.

Zaven stood, dusting himself off. "Then we wouldn't be having this tiresome conversation." He met Lux's eyes.

They stood there for a long moment, neither backing down.

Then Lux clicked his tongue. "Stay away from the mortal, Zaven," he warned before vanishing in a puff of smoke.

Though he never met his father, and he rarely, if ever, saw his mother, he never treated his familiars like the parents they were. They had raised him from the day he hatched, but that was their duty then. Now they served as his guardians and helpers. Perhaps he should at least treat them better than he did.

CHAPTER 9

Airlia's basket was heavy with meats, cheeses, and bread as she made her way home from the village, the setting sun casting long shadows through the dense trees. The air was thick with the scent of damp earth, and the quiet hum of evening insects filled the space between the rustling leaves. She felt exhausted but content—her near-drowning days before had left her shaken, but the warmth of life had gradually returned to her, even if she still did not understand the presence that had pulled her from the river's grasp.

Her cottage came into view, the chimney standing proud against the sky—but something felt wrong. The door, slightly ajar, moved just enough in the breeze to send a chill up her spine.

"Father?" she called, stepping inside.

Silence.

The fire had burned low, embers barely pulsing under a thin layer of ash. Her breath hitched. He should have stoked it by now. The weight in her basket suddenly felt unbearable, and she let it drop to the floor as she rushed into his room.

There, slumped in his chair by the window, was her father. Unmoving.

Airlia's heart stopped before hammering back to life in frantic bursts. "No," she whispered, her legs buckling beneath her as she reached out, her fingers barely grazing the cold skin of his hand.

The world around her collapsed into hushed stillness—except for the river. In the distance, through the open window, she could hear it murmuring, as if calling to her once more.

She swallowed, her chest tightening against the weight of grief. The entity that had saved her had felt like nothing she had ever known—its touch, its existence, lingering even now. Did it mean something? Had it warned her?

She closed her eyes, pressing her forehead against her father's cold fingers.

Airlia's breath came in short, uneven gasps, her fingers trembling as they traced the contours of her father's lifeless hand. They had always been warm—calloused from years of work, steady in a way that anchored her even when the world felt as if it were slipping away beneath her feet.

A sound escaped her, barely more than a whisper—raw, broken. The walls of the cottage, once so familiar, now closed in around her, suffocating in their silence. Shadows stretched long across the floor as the last light of day bled through the open window.

Beyond the trees, the river whispered.

She shivered, her mind pulling her back to that morning. The rushing water, the weightless sensation as she had been dragged under—the sheer terror that had wrapped around her like a vice. And then… the presence.

It had been there. Unseen. Wordless. But she had felt it, stronger than anything she had ever known. It had pulled her back, steadied her, saved her.

She swallowed hard, forcing herself to take in air.

Had it known? Had it warned her?

At the window, Airlia saw the last light of day paint the horizon in gold. The river's murmur wove itself into the silence, wrapping around her, pressing against the edges of her grief.

Gently, she leaned forward, pressing her forehead against her father's knuckles again. "I'm sorry," she whispered, barely more than a breath.

The wind shifted, cool air brushing against her cheeks like the lightest touch of fingers.

Eldrin approached the cottage with careful steps, the scent of turned earth and crushed herbs thick in the cooling air. He had just stepped past the threshold when he saw her—Airlia, crumpled beside her father's chair, shoulders shaking with silent grief.

For a moment, he hesitated, unwilling to intrude on something so raw, so unbreakable. But then, as though sensing him, she lifted her gaze.

Her eyes were red, swollen, hollow.

Eldrin swallowed and knelt beside her. "Airlia…" His voice was gentle, uncertain.

She did not speak. Her fingers curled into her father's tunic, gripping the fabric as though it could anchor her to something she was already losing.

Without another word, Eldrin reached out, his hand resting lightly on her back. She shuddered beneath his touch, but did not pull away.

Hours passed in silence before she whispered. "I don't know what to do." Her voice was fragile, hardly there.

Eldrin glanced at the window, at the stretch of land beyond. "We'll lay him to rest," he said softly. "Behind the house where the wildflowers grow."

Airlia's breath hitched, and for a long moment, she simply stared at him. Then, slowly, she nodded.

Together, they worked in quiet reverence, digging into the earth beneath the towering oak tree, where her father had often sat in the afternoons before he fell ill, watching the sky shift with the seasons. The night deepened around them; the wind carrying whispers of the river through the trees.

When it was done, Airlia remained, kneeling beside the freshly turned soil, her fingers brushing over it as if she could still reach him.

Eldrin stood beside her, watching, waiting.

She let out a breath shivering with sorrow. "He would have liked it here."

Eldrin nodded. "He will always be here."

Airlia swallowed hard and lifted her head to the sky, where the stars blinked in quiet vigil.

The river whispered. Something listened.

CHAPTER 10

She was sitting at the edge of the partially submerged boat, the hem of her dress trailing in the water like ribbons of ink. Moonlight traced the curve of her shoulders, and droplets clung to her as though reluctant to let her go.

From the bank, Zaven watched, his jaw set, cloak trailing in the shallows like smoke.

Another delay.

He had felt her soul arrive the moment her breath fled—rippling across the boundary like a bell rung beneath the tide. And yet she resisted. Sat there. Waiting.

"I don't have time for this," he muttered to the river.

Souls were not meant to linger. His path was not built for negotiation. He was meant to guide, to collect. Ozmir did the coaxing, the comforting. Zaven simply ensured the flow did not stall. He was not built for softness.

He could feel it—the soul resisting, not out of defiance, but sorrow. She had not expected death, not like this. Not in the stillness after the storm, when the waves had quieted, and the air tasted like coming rain.

He stepped into the water, feet slicing through reflections, his presence darkening the shallows. The woman turned at the sound—a flicker of fear in her eyes. Not unusual. But still irritating.

"You know what I am," he said. "You know why I'm here."

She hugged her arms tighter around herself. "I thought death would be quieter."

Zaven arched a brow. "You're sitting in a boat held together by will and memory. You've already died. You're simply… late."

"I didn't mean to be," she said, voice shaking. "I just— someone should've come. My sister. My father. Someone."

Zaven clenched his jaw. The impulse rose to tell her the truth plainly: the river took what it pleased. The living mourned and moved on. Souls did not get reunions. They got silence, and then they got him.

But something held his tongue.

He looked at her more carefully now. Not the soul—just the way she curled into herself, trembling like a bird who did not yet realize the sky had shattered. She was not being defiant. She was trying not to break.

He sighed quietly.

"I wasn't supposed to come," he said at last. "My brother would've been kinder. He speaks to the lost as if they're still whole. I don't know how to do that."

She blinked. "Then why did you come?"

"Because you weren't moving. And I—" He paused, the words unfamiliar. "I didn't want you to drown in something worse than death. Not alone."

That silenced her. The fear on her face softened—not gone, but no longer flinching.

"You look like grief," she said after a moment.

Zaven paused. He did not dispute it.

"I'm only here to take you across," he said. "Not to frighten you."

"That's what the frightened always hear," she replied, but her voice lacked venom. It was wistful more than bitter. "Is it true? That once I go, I don't come back?"

He considered lying. Or at least cloaking the truth in poetry like Ozmir did, speaking of release, of peace, of memory like stardust sinking beneath the waves. But this woman—this soul—she was not asking for pretty illusions.

"It's not the same," he said. "The parts of you that mattered—what you loved, what loved you—they carry forward. But the rest stays here. It has to."

She went quiet, watching ripples coil around her submerged ankles. "I'm not ready."

Zaven knelt beside the boat, the river rising to meet his knees. The move felt unnatural. He was more accustomed to looming. But tonight, he made himself smaller.

"I know," he said. "You can take a little longer. I'll wait."

She blinked at him, confused. "You'll wait?"

"I'm not in a hurry," he said. "The dead don't outrun me."

A ghost of a smile flickered on her lips. Then, her shoulders trembled. Not with fear. With release.

She reached out—not quite touching him, but close. "Will it hurt?"

"No," he answered. "You've already survived the hardest part."

A breeze stirred the mist. She looked down at her hands, then back at him. "Will anyone remember me?"

It was the kind of question that used to annoy him. Pointless. Mortal. But now it only settled inside his chest like something delicate and wrong.

"They will," he said. "And if they don't, I will."

Her breath hitched. Then she nodded, just once, and stepped out of the boat. Her form glimmered faintly as it touched the river's current.

Zaven reached for her—not commanding, not pulling—just offering a hand.

And this time, when the soul took it, he did not feel like death incarnate.

He felt like something briefly human.

The river was quiet now. The ripples had stilled; the soul long since passed. In the silence, Zaven remained, crouched at the edge of the water where the reeds bent like mourners and moonlight pooled around his feet.

He should have left. His work was done. But his hands still remembered the weight of hers—light as mist, fragile as trust. She had stepped into the current without resistance, guided by words he had not meant to offer.

Words he did not even know he had.

Zaven dragged a hand down his face. It felt wrong. Not in the way the currents clung to him or the chill gnawing at his cloak—but what he had said. What he had meant.

"You will be remembered." *If they don't, I will.*

Where had that come from?

He was not Ozmir. Zaven did not cradle the broken. He did not promise what could not be kept. And yet, when her eyes had searched his—not with defiance or despair, but aching uncertainty—he had reached for kindness as if it were instinct. As if something in him remembered how.

He hated that. The vulnerability of it. The raw, shifting ache in his chest that had no name.

Was this how his brother carried it? The weight of compassion?

It was heavier than Zaven had imagined.

He stared into the river, watching the phantom shimmer where her soul had been. The place where her memory lingered—not out of magic, but out of consequence.

"I shouldn't have stayed," he muttered to the water.

But he had. And now the silence felt less like solitude… and more like shame.

Not because he had failed. But because, in that moment, he had wanted to be kind.

He clenched his fists, knuckles whitening as the mist curled tighter around him.

If the drowned began to see him not as a harbinger but as a comfort, what would that make him? What else would they expect? And worse, what else might he begin to want?

Zaven stood, the shadows wrapping themselves around his shoulders again.

He would return to the depths. Back to the places where his name was a whisper of fear, not welcomed.

Yet as he walked, he could still feel the echo of her fingers in his palm.

And that, he feared, would not leave him soon.

CHAPTER 11

The river was a living thing, restless and hungry, swollen beyond its banks from the recent storm. Its surface gleamed in the morning light, deceptively calm, concealing the treacherous currents below. Zaven lingered in the veil of the trees, a mere phantom watching from the shadows.

And just as before, Airlia had ventured too close. As if she did not care about the danger. Then again, it was possible that it was her fate to drown. She seemed to be drawn to the river.

He had known the moment she would fall.

Airlia waded carefully along the edge, her bare feet pressing against slick rock, hesitant yet unafraid. Zaven could see the quiet determination on her face—the same determination that had nearly cost her life before.

He had hoped she would have had the good sense to stay away from the river, but the girl was fearless.

The moment came fast.

Her foot slipped on the slick moss-covered rock, and in an instant, the river claimed her. There was a sharp gasp—then silence as the water swallowed her whole.

It would have been so easy to let it happen. He knew he should have. The thought that the dark-haired man who seemed to always be watching her would step in this time, but he was not close that day. And Zaven was already moving.

He barely disturbed the surface as he entered, the currents parting for him, for they knew him well. His arms found her struggling form beneath the roiling waters, and he pulled her free, carrying her back to the safety of the shore. There was no struggle as he carried her back, no sign that she had felt him, seen him. He remained unseen as he laid her gently onto the damp earth, watching as she gasped, her chest heaving, her fingers clawing at the ground for something real, something stable.

Airlia coughed, shivering, unaware of the phantom hands that had saved her. Unaware of the silent guardian who had done so before.

She would never know.

He stepped back, fading into the unseen—only to be met with a harsh scoff.

"Yer an absolute fool, ya know?"

The voice was familiar. Critical and unamused.

Zaven turned, and there, perched atop the exposed roots of an old tree, was Nox. The feline flicked her tail, her luminous blue eyes narrowed in exasperation.

"I thought we had an agreement," Nox continued, leaping down soundlessly. "Ya were supposed to let her be. Ya were supposed to stop saving her."

"You and Lux made that agreement. Not me," Zaven said, his voice as steady as ever. "And she would have drowned."

Nox let out a dry laugh. "Oh, please. Ya've said that before. And yet she keeps finding her way back to the river."

She stretched lazily, her sharp claws extending against the earth before retracting. Zaven was grateful that there were no other mortals around. He was having a discussion with a talking cat, not that mortals could understand her. The Nakaru appeared and sounded like ordinary cats unless one knew how to properly listen.

"Tell me, Zaven," Nox mused, her tone quieter now, almost curious. "How long do ya plan to keep this up? Ya know full well that ya shouldn't interfere with her destiny."

Zaven said nothing. His stare lingered on Airlia as she pressed a trembling hand to her chest. Her breathing evening out.

Nox's sigh was long—suffering. "Fine. Pretend ya don't care, as usual. But don't think I won't remind ya again the next time ya drag her out of the river." She turned, disappearing into the underbrush with one last remark thrown over her shoulder. "And Ozzy's lookin' for ya."

With a flick of her tail, Nox vanished into the shadows, leaving Zaven standing alone, watching over the girl he would never let slip away. His existence the only secret the river kept.

CHAPTER 12

The celestial halls were silent, save for the hum of energy pulsing through the marble columns. Zaven stood near one of the towering columns, arms crossed, brown eyes looking over to the viewing orb that showed the mortal realm below. He saw her—Airlia—being consoled in the arms of that stranger again, ignorant of the forces that pulled at her fate, of the hands that should have never intervened twice now. And yet, the thought of her drowning, of her life being snuffed out before its time, had sent him plunging into the waters without hesitation. Without thought.

Behind him, Ozmir stood stiffly, his silver robes whispering against the stone floor as he shifted his weight. He was the younger twin. Always viewed as weak—too gentle, too compassionate for a god. The others mocked him for it, scoffed at his kindness towards mortals, yet none dared to speak when Zaven was near. He shielded Ozmir for centuries, stepping in when cruel whispers turned to venom.

At last, Ozmir spoke, his voice quiet, hesitant. "You saved her again."

Zaven did not turn. He let out air slowly, methodically, trying to control the storm stirring in his chest. "She was drowning," he replied, his voice even.

"And she was meant to drown." His voice was firm, but still kind.

The words lingered, hanging like the weight of judgement itself. Zaven scoffed softly, tilting his head just enough to glance at his brother over his shoulder.

Zaven exhaled through his nose. His response was wry, edged with frustration. "You sound like the others."

Ozmir stiffened, as if struck. The others—the gods who belittled him for his softness, his quiet heart—they would speak of fate with cold certainty. But Ozmir was not like them.

And yet… Zaven said them anyway.

"I don't say it to be cruel," said Ozmir. He paused, then spoke softer, "I say it because I fear for you."

That caught Zaven's full attention. He turned, meeting Ozmir's gaze. His brother's blue eyes shone with something rare in the divine realm—genuine worry.

Ozmir pressed on, his voice steady, but imploring. "You know what happens to gods who intervene too much. You know how they talk about me, how they judge me. If they learn what you've done…"

A flicker of something unreadable crossed Zaven's face. It was an unfamiliar thing to be warned. He was the protector. The shield between Ozmir and the cruel, unyielding judgment of their kind. And yet now, the roles had shifted. Now Ozmir feared for him.

Zaven blew out sharply, the sound barely audible. He knew Ozmir was right. He knew the laws, the punishment that awaited gods who stepped too far beyond their purpose. And yet, when Airlia's life hung in the balance, when the waters pulled her under, he had not hesitated.

Not once.

"I don't care what they say," Zaven said, his voice low, firm.

Ozmir's face tightened—not with anger, but with something softer. Sorrow, perhaps. "You should."

Zaven did not answer. He merely turned away, looking once more at the viewing orb. The wind stirred across the celestial halls, carrying Ozmir's words like an omen, like something inevitable.

"Tell me, brother—what is it about this mortal that makes you defy our laws?"

Zaven opened his mouth, then stopped. The answer was simple. And yet, he could not voice it. He did not know what bound him to Airlia, what made her different from the others he watched pass from one realm to the next.

But Ozmir did. His voice was soft, almost pitying. "You care for her."

Zaven stiffened, and too quickly replied, "I do not."

Ozmir's silence was more damning than words. He studied Zaven like a creature doomed to fall, like a brother grasping at denial before the storm consumed him.

And with quiet certainty, Ozmir said, "Yes, you do."

Zaven continued to stare at the viewing orb. Airlia was in her cottage, safe—for now, but not alone. Why did he keep saving her? Why was he risking his immortality for her? She already had someone. Why did she matter so much to him? Did he truly care for the mortal?

Ozmir stepped beside him, voice softer now, more resigned. "You know how this ends."

Zaven clenched his jaw. He knew. He had seen it before—gods who forgot their place, who loved where they should not have, who were punished for daring to hold what was never meant to be theirs.

But knowing did not change what he felt.

And Zaven, despite every warning, did not wish to change.

CHAPTER 13

Drowned souls did not always stay silent. Some whispered, their voices carrying through the currents like broken fragments of memory. Others lamented, clinging to the weight of their final moments, grasping for the warmth they had lost. Zaven did not answer them. Their words were not meant for him.

He was merely their shepherd, guiding them beyond the threshold, to the place where Ozmir would greet them with endless patience and gentle words. Ozmir, ever the caretaker, cradled their grief, soothed their unraveling souls with quiet reassurances. It was his way, his nature. Zaven had never understood it.

Grief was grief. It did not need soft hands or whispered comforts. It only needed an end.

And yet, in the stillness between tides, in the empty stretches where the drowned drifted toward Ozmir's embrace, Zaven sometimes listened. Not because he wished to. Not because he cared. But because the voices gnawed at the edges of his solitude, filling the silence with half-spoken regrets, with unbidden echoes of longing.

He had never considered it loneliness before.

Had never thought of the weight in his chest as anything other than an inevitable part of his existence. He had accepted his place among the depths, his duty as the usher of drowned souls. There had never been anything more for him, nor had he sought it.

Until her.

Airlia did not belong in his world, did not belong in the realm of the drowned. She was alive, and relentless in her care of others—full of life, full of fight. She had no place among the shadows he walked. And yet he found himself watching, drawn to the way she moved through the world, the way she resisted the very forces that had claimed countless others before her.

With his help, of course.

It was careless, indulgent. A foolish distraction.

But the souls still spoke, and he still listened.

Perhaps that was his mistake.

The river churned in uneasy swells, its surface flecked with moonlight, its depths shifting with unseen currents. Zaven moved through the shallows, mist clinging to the edges of his cloak, the scent of damp earth thick in the air. He had been searching for some time now. Even Lux and Nox were unable to find it. The soul was near, hovering between the reeds, reluctant.

It had not come willingly.

He drew to a stop, his gaze settling on the fragile shimmer in the fog—small, hesitant, curled inward like something still clinging to warmth that was no longer there.

"You should not linger." His voice was quiet, but firm, cutting through the hush of the water. "It's time."

A tremor passed through the mist. The soul flinched, shrinking into itself.

"I can't," it whispered. "I lost my mother's hand. I wasn't supposed to let go."

Zaven let out an angry breath, pressing his fingers against his temple. This was not his task—this was Ozmir's domain. Ozmir was the patient one, the gentle one, the god who murmured soft assurances to hesitant souls. Zaven was not a healer. He was merely the passage between what was and what must be.

And yet the child did not move.

He stepped closer, his presence looming, deliberate. "You cannot stay."

The soul trembled, curling tighter, its form quivering at the edges like candlelight on the verge of dying out. "She's waiting," it mumbled, pleading. "She has to be."

Zaven knew better.

He had seen the mother at the river's edge, had felt the echo of her grief in the tides. She had screamed until her voice had frayed, had plunged her hands into the water as if she might pull her child from the depths with nothing but raw desperation. She had not yet given up.

But she would.

And the child—this fragile thing before him—was already gone.

A flash of irritation stirred in his chest. This was taking too long. He did not have patience for whimpering souls.

They had drowned. Their stories had ended. It was their fate.

Yet still, the child did not move.

Zaven clenched his jaw. And then, against his better judgment, he said, "She will remember you."

The words felt foreign on his tongue, unnatural. His role was not to comfort, but the soul remained, stubborn in its sorrow, trembling in its final refusal.

"She will carry you," he continued, the weight of his voice settling like mist on water. "In every breath, in every quiet moment."

The child's soul stilled. It was listening.

"You are not lost." The thought unsettled him. He was the god of drowned souls. Lost things were his domain. And yet here, in this fragile exchange, he found himself grasping for something beyond his purpose.

The soul wavered. Then, slowly, it moved.

It stepped forward, releasing its grip on the mortal world, on the impossible hope that its mother would find it.

Zaven did not sigh in relief. He merely turned, guiding the small soul toward the waiting dark, toward the place where Ozmir would take its sorrow and cradle it with tenderness Zaven did not know how to give.

He was not soft. He was not gentle. But tonight, perhaps, he had understood.

CHAPTER 14

Churning, the river's clear waters lapped against the shore with an unnatural hunger. Mist clung to the surface like the breath of something waiting beneath. Airlia carefully walked along the river's edge, picking different plants as she did. When she looked up, she saw it.

It was the most beautiful, albeit strange-looking, black horse she had ever seen. She crouched, reaching toward the creature as it stood knee-deep in the shallows—it was sleek and impossibly beautiful, its coat slick with moisture. It blinked at her, eyes wide and inviting, as if expecting her touch.

Her fingers brushed damp—scales?

A sudden force wrenched her back. The world tilted—water, sky, reeds blurring as she was hauled away. She gasped in shock as she hit her head on a rock. Relief filled her as the last thing she saw was a figure diving in after her. A strong grip encircled her waist, the same firm but unyielding grasp she had felt before.

"You have a habit of doing this," came the voice, low and rough, edged with something undetectable.

Still, she felt safe as the darkness took her.

Once she regained consciousness, the strange but beautiful horse was grazing next to her, and just for a moment, she thought it was what saved her. Then she remembered that someone had spoken to her before she blacked out. And her head was elevated on someone's lap. She looked up to see a pair of eyes the color of the finest ale caught in sunlight peering down at her, studying her, but neither unkind nor wholly warm. His short, dark hair appeared wet as it caught the weak sunlight.

Though she immediately regretted it, she bolted upright and quickly moved away from the stranger, startling the horse briefly. The stranger had an almost worried look in his dark amber eyes when she winced in pain.

She narrowed hers. "W-who are you?" She touched the back of her head and drew blood.

"A friend. I won't hurt you," he replied casually.

"Did you save me?"

He inclined his head slightly. "Yes, I hope that's all right." His face scrunched up at his words.

It was such an odd thing for him to say. "Of course it is!" Again, she winced in pain. He seemed amused. "Why wouldn't it be?"

He looked up at the sky briefly, as if deciding how he would answer her. "Mother would be angry if she knew I interfered with a soul's destiny, but he," he pointed to the horse, "said you were good, but he said he was hurt and couldn't save you himself." He narrowed his eyes at the horse. "He was obviously faking, since he's better now."

For a moment, she thought she had died as she sat and stared at the man who talked to horses with scales and about the destiny of souls. Odd. She thought he was odd. Especially with the random patches of black scales that had an iridescent blue sheen to them and looked like gemstones. His hair still appeared wet, but he was dry, and she could see no water on the strands. But there was something else about him—something weighty, something ethereal—that made her stomach twist in ways she did not fully understand.

"I'm sorry. Did you say the horse told you I was good?"

The man smiled. "He's a kelpie, not a horse."

"A what?"

"A kelpie. They look like horses, but they're not. I can talk to them."

He seemed so proud of something so peculiar. He was handsome, and looked young—around her age—but the look in his eyes made him seem much older. "And what are you that you can talk to strange horses?"

"Kelpie," he corrected. "And I told you, I'm a friend. You're very pretty."

Both their faces scrunched up this time.

"And you're a very odd… friend."

He frowned at that. "Well, that's not very nice to say. I saved your life."

At that, she flushed red. "You're right, I'm sorry. Thank you so much for that."

"My name's Zaven. What's yours?"

Again, she narrowed her eyes at him. "Airlia," she replied. She suspected that he already knew her name and had been watching her. "Zaven?"

He nodded. "Yes. Zaven Lareceun."

It was not just a name. It carried weight, something edged and certain. She rolled it over in her mind before speaking it aloud again. "Zaven," she echoed. It suited him—intense, enigmatic, like something carved in stone.

A silence settled between them, heavy but not hostile. She shifted, brushing damp earth from her palms before offering a nod. "Well… thank you. Again."

His gaze flickered downward, as if uncertain how to accept her gratitude. Was he blushing?

Her eyes darted toward the river, where the horse—kelpie—now stood half-dissolved, its form unraveling like fog beneath the surface. "It wasn't real," she said, more to herself than to him.

Zaven's jaw tightened. "It was real enough to drown you."

She exhaled, the weight of the moment pressing against her ribs. He was not wrong. And for the third time, she had been saved by him. This stranger. This odd presence that lingered just outside the periphery of understanding.

Her pulse steadied, though the tension remained. "Three times now," she murmured, meeting his gaze.

Another pause. He could have warned her. Could have chastised her for recklessness. But he did not.

He only nodded, as if he were accepting something inevitable.

She did not know what to make of him. Something about him unsettled her—not in fear, but in the way he presented himself, as if he was not entirely of this world.

She was not sure she liked that. But for now, she owed him.

And that, at least, was undeniable.

They both turned toward the woods when they heard a noise—a twig snapping underfoot.

"Airlia?" came Eldrin's voice as he came into view.

She heard a tsking sound come from Zaven, but when she turned back to him, he was gone.

"Airlia, you're soaking wet. Are you all right?" he asked worriedly as he knelt down beside her.

She opened her mouth to tell him about Zaven and the kelpie, but decided not to. He would probably think her mad for mentioning what had happened. "I fell in the river again," she decided. "But I'm fine now. Just a little sore, that's all."

"Your head is bleeding," he said firmly. "How exactly did you get out with such an injury?"

Airlia smiled at the suspicious look in his deep brown eyes. They were not as lovely as Zaven's. "There's two of you now," she giggled drunkenly, then collapsed into his arms.

CHAPTER 15

Airlia sensed him before she saw him.

It was always the same—a shift in the air, a quiet disturbance, as though the space around her rippled in recognition of something unseen. She did not turn immediately, instead letting the moment settle as she focused on the small scraped knee before her. The child sniffled but did not cry, watching with wide, curious eyes as Airlia worked with gentle precision, wrapping a strip of cloth securely over the wound.

"There," she murmured, tying the final knot. "All better."

The girl tested her leg, then beamed, running off to her mother with a triumphant grin. Airlia exhaled, rolling her shoulders before lifting her head toward the treeline.

He was there again. Zaven.

The edge of dusk blurred around him, the deepening shadows folding him into their embrace. He had not spoken to her since that moment by the river, but she saw him more often now—always on the edges, always watching. It was not unnerving exactly. Just... peculiar.

She tilted her head. "You could come closer, you know."

A pause. He stood as if tethered by an invisible boundary, unwilling or unable to breach it. Then, with deliberate slowness, he stepped forward.

"You do this often," he said—not a question, more of an observation, his voice low, like distant thunder.

She flexed her fingers, rubbing the faint warmth of sunlight into her skin. "Yes," she said simply. "People need tending."

His eyes flickered briefly toward the villagers, toward the rhythm of their lives—the laughter of children, the murmured prayers of elders, the slow, unbroken cycle of hearth and home. He stood apart from it all, though not with disdain. With distance. A separation that was ingrained, unshaken.

"You watch them a lot," she remarked.

Zaven said nothing.

Airlia let the silence linger, studying him with quiet patience. Loneliness clung to him, thick and invisible, but no less tangible. She could feel it—not just as an absence, but as a hollow ache, like something abandoned within a vast, empty hall.

She was not sure why she reached for him. But she did.

"Do you ever get tired?" she asked softly.

His brow furrowed, his eyes fixed on hers. "Tired?"

She nodded, folding her arms against the evening's creeping chill. "Of being alone."

The silence stretched longer this time. He did not shift, did not speak. But she saw the flicker, the briefest crack in the rigid wall he had built around himself.

"I don't—" His voice faltered, jaw tightening.

Airlia smiled, just barely. "You don't have to say it. I can tell."

She expected him to pull away. To vanish the way he always did. But he did not. He lingered, staring at her as if trying to decipher some puzzle he had not expected to be given.

She reached for him again, his hand, just briefly—a gesture, light and fleeting, meant only to assure.

"If you ever want company," she murmured, "you don't have to stay on the edges."

Then she let go.

Zaven looked down at the place where her fingers had brushed against his. He did not move. Did not speak. But he did not leave either.

And maybe, just maybe, that was something.

CHAPTER 16

The morning air was crisp, carrying the scent of damp earth and the whisper of leaves shifting overhead. Sunlight trickled through the canopy in fractured beams, casting dappled patterns against the forest floor where herbs grew in clusters, curling up from the soil like fragile green fingers.

Airlia crouched among them, brushing her fingertips along the leaves of a familiar sprig, the texture soft and pliant. She plucked a handful with care, tucking them into the small woven basket at her side.

Zaven stood a few feet away, utterly lost. She bit back a grin.

His posture was rigid, shoulders tense, as if he were handling something far more dangerous than simple flora.

He held a bundle of plants in his grasp—long-stemmed, thick-rooted, tangled together as though he had yanked them from the ground indiscriminately.

Airlia rose, stepping toward him. "You're just ripping them up like weeds."

"They are weeds," he said flatly.

She laughed, the sound light as the breeze threading through the trees. "Not all of them." She pointed to his hand, plucking a single stem from the mess he had gathered. "This one, yes. But this?" She held up another, its scent strong and medicinal. "This is bloodroot. It's a good antiseptic."

Zaven glanced toward the plant as if attempting to decipher its purpose. He said nothing, but Airlia caught the faint furrow of his brow—the smallest sign of interest.

She crouched again, gesturing for him to kneel beside her. He did, albeit stiffly, watching as she carefully unearthed a root without breaking its fibers.

"My father taught me this," she murmured, brushing loose soil from the plant. "You have to be gentle, or you'll ruin the potency."

Zaven studied her hands, then the plants, then his own clumsy attempt at gathering them. She could almost see the realization forming behind his silence—that there was a method, a purpose, something beyond simply pulling things from the ground.

Airlia smiled and held the bundle toward him. "Try again."

He hesitated, then reached forward, his movements deliberate this time, more measured. He pulled, testing the resistance, feeling the earth yield beneath his touch. The stem remained intact.

The root was clean.

Airlia nodded approvingly. "Better."

Zaven breathed out—not quite relief, but something close to understanding. He said nothing, but she noticed he did not drop the plant. Instead, he turned it over in his palm, absorbing its weight and scent, as if committing it to memory.

She watched him for a moment longer, seeing the faintest crack in his usual detachment, the quiet intrigue woven into his movements.

She liked this—seeing him among the living, among something simple and real, even if he did not quite belong. And maybe, just maybe, he was starting to learn that he did not always have to stand on the edges.

As Airlia continued to move between the thickets, her basket grew heavier with sprigs of bloodroot, stinging nettle, and goldenseal. Beside her, Zaven handled the plants with cautious precision. His movements were more measured than before, though still stiff, as if the simple act of gathering herbs remained foreign to him.

She caught him furrowing his brow as he rolled a stem between his fingers, inspecting the delicate veins of the leaf. A smile tugged at her lips. "You don't have to study them like they're riddles," she teased, reaching out to pluck the plant from his grasp. "Just feel the weight of them. Know how they breathe."

Zaven's eyes flicked toward her, unreadable but attentive, as if committing her words to memory.

The moment lingered—quiet, easy.

Then the stillness broke.

Airlia heard the approaching footsteps before she saw him. A purposeful stride, light yet firm against the ground, the sound of someone used to moving through the wilds.

She turned just as Eldrin pushed through the underbrush, bow slung over his shoulder, a brace of rabbits hanging from his belt.

The moment his eyes landed on Zaven, they darkened. He halted. "Who the hell is this?"

Zaven straightened, but remained silent, his presence shifting, withdrawing into something more guarded.

Airlia sighed, brushing dirt from her hands. "We're picking herbs."

Eldrin's gaze moved from her to Zaven, his jaw tightening. "We?" His tone was accusatory. "You didn't say you'd be out here with someone." His voice was edged now, firm but not loud—his hunter's instincts kicking in, assessing. "He doesn't look like he comes from our village."

She felt Zaven tense beside her, though his expression remained unreadable.

Airlia sighed again. "He's helping."

Eldrin looked at Zaven's hands—his awkward grip on the herbs, the stiff way he held them. "Helping?" he sneered. "He looks like he's never touched a plant in his life."

Airlia's lips parted, but before she could reply, Eldrin took another step forward, his stance shifting. Protective. Wary. "You shouldn't be out here alone with a stranger," he said softly. "He's strange-looking. What do you even know about him?"

Zaven spoke, his voice calm but flat. "Enough to know how to gather bloodroot."

Eldrin narrowed his eyes. "That's not an answer."

Something in the air thickened—unspoken tension curling between them.

Airlia glanced between them, frustration tightening in her chest. Eldrin was not unjustified—he was cautious, protective, always scanning for unseen threats. But Zaven was not a threat. He was just… something else. Something harder to explain.

"I trust him," she said simply.

Again, Eldrin's jaw tightened. The weight of unspoken words pressed against the space between them, thick enough to suffocate.

She did not want to say it like this, but she knew there was no other way. "You're wrong about him," she said quietly.

Eldrin frown. "I don't think I am."

Airlia tightened her grip on the basket. "He saved me."

Eldrin's head snapped toward her. "What?"

She met his glare. "At the river. When—" She hesitated, suddenly feeling the heaviness of the memories. "When I almost drowned. He pulled me out each time."

Eldrin stared at her, his look shifting from shock to something harsher—something she could not quite name.

"You never told me that," he said, voice quieter now.

"I didn't think—" she sighed, shaking her head. "I don't know. I didn't know what to make of him then."

"And now you do?"

She hesitated. "I'm trying to."

Eldrin growled. "You don't know what he is, Airlia. You don't know where he came from, or why he's even here. People like that—people who appear out of nowhere—they don't just show up without a reason."

"He's not dangerous," she said, softer this time.

"You don't know that," Eldrin countered, frustration creeping into his voice. "Saving you doesn't mean he isn't something you shouldn't be afraid of."

Airlia exhaled, shaking her head. "I'm not afraid."

"Look at him! He's not even human!"

The words landed heavier than she expected. There was no malice in them, no cruelty—just unshaken certainty.

She looked at Eldrin then, really looked at him. At the hunter who had always protected, always watched, always been one to stand between her and whatever unseen dangers lurked beyond the village. She understood him, understood why he felt that way. But she also understood Zaven in a way Eldrin never could.

She swallowed hard. "I still trust him. With my life."

Eldrin's mouth pressed into a thin line.

The silence stretched long between them.

Then Eldrin turned his attention to Zaven. And for the first time, Airlia felt the weight of standing between two sides—one known, one unknown, both unmoving.

The tension hung thick in the air, pressing against the quiet hum of the forest.

Zaven stood still, his usual unreadable mask in place, yet something in his posture had shifted—subtle, barely noticeable, but present. He watched Eldrin with a steady, calculating look, neither retreating nor engaging.

Eldrin, however, was not as composed.

His grip tightened around the handle of his hunting knife; his jaw locked. "I don't know what you are," he said, voice low, edged. "But I know I don't trust you."

Airlia stiffened beside him. "Eldrin—"

"You just appeared," Eldrin snapped. "Out of nowhere. And now you follow her? Stay close to her? You saved her, sure, but that doesn't mean I don't see what you're doing."

Zaven raised a brow, his expression unwavering. "And what am I doing?"

Eldrin stepped closer. "I don't know yet. But I know that if you ever hurt her—if you ever give me a reason to think she isn't safe with you—I'll put you down before you get the chance."

A biting silence fell between them.

Airlia's breath caught, a mixture of shock and frustration rising within her. "Eldrin, stop."

Zaven did not flinch. He remained unmoved, staring at Eldrin with something that was not quite amusement, or quite indifference. "I don't need your permission to be here," he said calmly.

"And I don't need a reason to make sure you stay away from her."

Airlia stepped between them then, pushing lightly against Eldrin's chest. "Enough," she said firmly. "He has done nothing to deserve this."

Eldrin's eyes flashed with something uncertain, but his grip on his knife did not loosen.

Zaven tilted his head slightly, observing the way she placed herself in front of Eldrin's anger. Not for him, but for herself. For the choice she had already made.

Slowly, deliberately, he turned his gaze back to Eldrin. "If you want to threaten me," he murmured, low and unimpressed, "at least make it interesting."

Eldrin stiffened.

Airlia narrowed her eyes at both of them, exhaling intensely before shaking her head again. "This is ridiculous." She grabbed her basket, turning away. "I have work to do." She did not wait for either of them to follow.

But after a moment, Zaven did.

Eldrin remained where he stood, knife still in hand, watching them disappear into the trees.

CHAPTER 17

The village had quieted, the distant hum of voices fading into the evening air as the weight of the day settled over the rooftops. The scent of herbs lingered in Airlia's small healing space, mixing with the faint metallic tang of blood. Zaven stood near the doorway, his company a steady weight—unwelcomed by most, misunderstood by all. The villagers still whispered about him after he showed up with her one day. They were wary of the stranger who lingered in shadows, the one who did not look or seem wholly human.

And yet, here he was. Here with her.

A sharp gasp broke the silence. The wounded man on the table writhed, blood slick against his skin, the deep gash along his ribs refusing to clot. Airlia pressed a cloth to the wound, but it was failing—he was losing too much.

She felt Zaven shift beside her. "You won't stop it in time."

Her pulse thudded. She knew that. But she was not ready to lose him. He had a wife and two children who worried about him.

Zaven's fingers ghosted over the wound, barely touching the skin. A breath, a moment—and then the blood slowed.

Airlia watched, stunned, as water shimmered against his fingertips, weaving across the torn flesh in delicate, curling threads, forming a barrier long enough for her to stitch the wound closed.

Her hands moved quickly, precise. Zaven did not speak. When she was done, he withdrew. The water melted away. The farmer stirred, weak but alive.

Airlia exhaled loudly, brushing damp hair from her brow, then turned to face Zaven fully. "How—" she began, but the words faltered. She already knew the answer. Not fully, but enough. She knew that creatures that appeared human and had magic existed in the world outside her village. But to see one, to know them, was different.

He studied her, something unreadable flashing in his eyes. Then he spoke. "I'm not what they think I am." His voice was quieter than usual, like a confession weighted by centuries. "I'm not a demon. I'm a god of death. You can tell no one of this."

The words settled between them, shifting everything and yet... nothing at all. Airlia did not move. She let the truth sink in, let the weight of it press against the trust she had already built. "You shepherd the dead?" she asked.

His look darkened. "The drowned. Those the water takes," he clarified.

She swallowed, watching him, searching for anything in his expression that would make her question what she already knew—that he was not cruel, was not malicious, was not something to be feared the way others believed.

He had saved her. He had lingered. He had helped.

"Then why save me?" she asked.

A pause. He turned away. "I don't know."

But Airlia saw something in his stance, in the way he kept himself distant, yet never far.

She let the quiet linger between them as she reached for the damp cloth beside her, running her fingers over the frayed edge. "I dream about the water sometimes," she admitted.

Zaven's eyes snapped back to hers.

She smiled faintly, but there was no humor in it. "Not in the way you might think. I dream about sinking, about the cold pressing against my skin. But I'm not afraid of drowning. I'm afraid of losing myself."

He studied her, his look shifting, but he did not speak.

She sighed, brushing stray hairs from her brow. "And then there are the dreams that feel more like wishes. I want to heal people. To know that I've done something real, something that matters. But some nights, I wonder if it will ever be enough."

Zaven was silent for a long moment. Then, slowly, he spoke. "It is enough."

She met his eyes.

"You matter," he said simply.

Something inside her tightened—not in pain, but in recognition. And then, softly, she reached for his hand, her fingers brushing against his as gently as a passing breeze. "You don't have to be alone," she murmured.

He did not pull away.

She offered the faintest smile again. "I mean it, Zaven. You don't have to stand in the dark all the time."

For a long moment, he said nothing. Then he slowly breathed out—soft, like something long held finally slipping free. "You are stubborn," he said.

"So I've been told."

Something sparked between them, something quiet yet strong. The feel of unspoken truths, of unasked questions, and of things neither of them knew to name.

He stepped closer, his presence shifting, like a tide moving forward instead of retreating. And with quiet certainty, Airlia tilted her chin. The first brush of his lips against hers was tentative, uncertain, as if he was not sure this was something he was allowed to do. But Airlia met him halfway, the coolness of his breath mixing with the warmth of hers, the slow sureness of a moment neither of them could take back.

The light brush of his tongue against her lips, entreating entrance, was soft. She parted her lips and let him in, her tongue meeting his in a dance of passion. She felt the gentle press of his fingers on her hips as he drew her closer to him. His body was firm and felt strong. But it was also cold, and she did not feel a pulse. The feel of his erection brought her out of her observation and back to what he was making her feel. Suddenly, she forgot what she had been thinking about.

When they pulled away, the world felt different.

Zaven's gaze lingered on her, something barely spoken, resting behind his eyes.

Airlia smiled, breathless but steady. "You really don't have to keep saving me," she whispered.

His lips barely curved. "I think you make it difficult."

She laughed, shaking her head, and for the first time, Zaven did not feel like the god standing on the outside. For the first time, he was letting himself belong. The weight between them felt lighter.

CHAPTER 18

The celestial tides churned restlessly against the shore, the rhythmic pull of the water carrying unspoken tension between the twin gods standing at its edge. Moonlight scattered over the waves in broken fragments, silver threads weaving across the surface, illuminating their figures like specters caught between realms.

Zaven stood rigid, watching the sea with a quiet intensity, his arms crossed over his chest, jaw tight. Ozmir, his mirror yet his opposite, paced before him, movements sharp, his face edged with something between frustration and hurt.

"I see your familiars more than I see you," Ozmir muttered, his blond hair catching the dim glow of the night. "They do your work for you."

Zaven said nothing.

Ozmir's lip curled. "You used to be there—watching, guiding. You were never the one who shirked duty." He shook his head, brows furrowing deeper. "Now, I look for you and find nothing. Only whispers of your name. Only your familiars lingering in your place."

Zaven breathed out abruptly. "The job gets done."

"That's not the point." Ozmir's voice had lost its edge now, but not its weight. There was something fractured beneath it—something unsettled. "The dead call for you, and yet you're elsewhere. You're with her."

The name was not spoken, but it did not need to be.

Zaven stiffened.

Ozmir tilted his head, watching the shift in his twin's posture. "You haven't denied it."

Zaven clenched his jaw, turning away toward the horizon, toward the place where the sea met the sky in a boundless expanse—toward anywhere but his brother. "It changes nothing," he grumbled.

Ozmir scoffed. "It changes everything." He took a step forward, his aura pressing against the space between them. "She's mortal, Zaven. She is not meant for you."

"Were you not the one that said I needed to empathize more, and to stop being so cold and distant?" Zaven countered.

Ozmir narrowed his eyes, studying his twin, searching for the unraveling threads that had pulled him toward something fragile, something human. Something that should never have taken root.

"She's made you weak."

Zaven's head snapped toward him, dark eyes flashing like a storm brewing beneath the surface. "Careful."

Ozmir did not flinch. "It's the truth."

"I thought you wanted me to be more like you," Zaven snapped.

The words struck deeper than any blade. Zaven could see it in his brother's eyes.

Silence coiled between them, thick and pulsing.

Then Ozmir exhaled slowly, his tone shifting—not gentler, but quieter, more deliberate. "Does Mother know?"

Zaven stilled.

Ozmir held his gaze. "She won't be pleased."

Something in the air crackled—a shift, abrupt and unseen, rippling outward like a disturbance in the tide.

Zaven's stare was cold now, colder than it had been before. "You wouldn't."

Ozmir lifted his chin, studying the hardened lines of his twin's expression, weighing the depth of his attachment, the extent of his defiance. "Wouldn't I?"

The quiet stretched, pressing against them, heavy with unspoken threads and unbreakable bonds.

Then, without another word, without another breath, Zaven stepped back, his presence withdrawing, pulling inward into something distant. Something colder.

He turned, and then he left.

Ozmir remained, standing alone on the shifting shore, the waves curling at his feet like whispers of something lost.

And the sea carried the weight of their fracture into the dark.

CHAPTER 19

Their voices carried through the evening air, bitter and cutting. Airlia stood at her cottage door, arms crossed over her chest, frustration tightening in her throat as the men before her continued their tirade. Their words were not new. Their contempt was not unexpected. But tonight, it weighed heavier.

"You think you're safe with him?" one of them scoffed, arms thrown up in exasperation. "Whatever he is, he's not like us."

Another, older, sneered. "People say he's cursed."

Airlia gritted her teeth. "You don't know him."

"And you do?" The first man let out a dry laugh. "Is that what you think? That you've tamed whatever demon lurks in his skin? He's got you bewitched, girl."

Before she could snap back, the air shifted.

The crackling tension thickened, like the sudden pressure before a storm.

Zaven had arrived.

The men noticed him immediately, their bodies stiffening, their words faltering as his tall figure loomed at the edge of the clearing, his authority consuming the space as effortlessly as the tide swallowing the shore. He said nothing—he did not need to. His silence was heavier than their threats.

The first man took a wary step back, trying to mask his unease with bravado. "What? You come to stand behind her now?" He scoffed, though it lacked confidence. "Acting like some guardian?"

Zaven's expression was indecipherable, but his voice, low and edged, carried without effort. "I don't stand behind anyone."

The way he said it—calm, unwavering—sent a visible chill through them.

The third man paled somewhat, but held his stance. "You—" He swallowed hard. "You should leave."

Zaven tilted his head ever so slightly, as if he was amused by the demand. "I won't be the one leaving."

There was no threat. Not explicit. Not spoken. But the men felt it anyway.

The silence stretched out before them, thick and unyielding. And then, one by one, they withdrew, muttering curses to themselves, retreating into the night like creatures unwilling to challenge something beyond their understanding.

Airlia breathed out, shaking her head. "Idiots."

Zaven remained still, his expression still unreadable. He had not looked at her yet, had not shifted his stance. It was not until the last of the men disappeared beyond the treeline that she noticed—his shoulders were tense, his jaw locked. He was not just cold. He was fuming.

She frowned, stepping closer. "What happened?"

Zaven did not answer immediately. Then, gradually, he let out a lungful of air, the tension in his frame barely loosening. "Ozmir."

Airlia studied him, waiting for him to continue. When he did not, she stepped forward more. "Tell me."

His brow furrowed slightly, as if struggling with something unspoken. Then he spoke. "He thinks I've abandoned my duty. That I've... weakened." His jaw tightened. "He threatened to tell our mother."

Airlia absorbed his words, her chest tightening slightly at the weight of them. This was not just an argument. This was something deeper—something rooted in forces older than herself, possibly older than him.

She reached for his hand, gently curling her fingers around his wrist. "You're not weak," she said quietly.

He did not pull away.

She smiled faintly, squeezing lightly. "Come inside. I'll make you tea."

Zaven raised a brow, his voice dipping into something wry. "Tea."

Airlia laughed softly. "It helps. Or, if not that... just let me be here." She tilted her head, warmth threading through her expression. "Let me ease the weight of this."

For the first time that night, he looked at her fully. And gradually, wordlessly, he let her lead him inside.

Once they were inside, he descended on her. Before she could protest, his lips had claimed hers. His kiss was fierce, demanding. She found she could spend a lifetime kissing him. When she was gasping for breath, he pulled away and kissed her along her throat, crushing her body to his. His hands slid along her throat, and then to the nape of her neck. He buried his long fingers in her hair as he suckled on her pulse point.

Then he pulled at her clothes, and she hardly noticed as they came gliding off and pooling to the floor. As he explored her bare skin, she noticed, for the second time, how cold his touch was. And he still had no pulse.

Snapping out of the spell of his kiss, she lightly pushed him back. "Zaven, wait," she said breathlessly.

He ignored her request as he drew her back to him.

Again, she pushed him away, but with more force. "Zaven, stop," she demanded.

This time, she had his attention.

His brow furrowed in confusion. "I thought you wanted to ease the weight of my tension?"

She flushed red briefly. "Yes, with tea."

"I do not want tea. I want you," he admitted.

"Oh," she gasped.

His eyes darkened with lust. "Your bedchamber. Where is it?" he growled.

She pointed silently in the direction he requested. When she turned back to him, his mouth was on hers again. He hoisted her up as they kissed, her legs wrapping around his waist. She had forgotten what she had wanted to say to him before, the heat of his passion distracting her.

He carried her to her room and laid her down gently on the bed. As he removed his tunic and trousers, he stared down at her naked body, then blushed when she stared back. His erection stood tall and proud, his need evident. She covered herself with her hands, her skin turning a bright red.

He shook his head as he approached, removing her hands. "Don't hide from me."

When he climbed on top of her, she shivered from the contact. Again, she blushed.

"Why are you so cold?" she asked, her tone nervous. "Why can't I feel your heartbeat?"

He avoided her gaze then. "Because it does not beat. Ever." He turned to her. "Not only do I shepherd the dead, I am one of them in a way," he explained. "I have flesh and power, but that is all that separates me from them."

"Do you not feel?" she wondered.

"I can," he replied. "Does knowing all this frighten you?"

She shook her head, her hands reaching up to touch his face. He closed his eyes, as if he were enjoying the warmth her hands brought. She brushed her fingers lightly across the patch of scales at his temple, just below his hairline.

"Why do you have scales?"

"I am a dragon. We all have them," he admitted, opening his eyes to watch as she inspected him.

She marveled at their texture and the iridescent blue sheen they had. "They're beautiful," she said, almost in a whisper.

He leaned down and kissed her again. This time, it was soft, tender. Then his mouth traveled down to her neck, on to her collarbone, before finding its way to the soft, supple mounds of her breasts. Again, she shivered when the coolness of his saliva touched her bare nipple as he wrapped his tongue around the protruding nub. Her nipple perked up under his attention. She arched into him when he lightly bit down on her. The sensation was foreign, sending jolts of electricity through her.

She did not know when her eyes closed, but when she opened them again, he was watching her as he kissed his way down the flat of her navel. His tongue circled around the small closing, slowly, methodically. Then he moved on, further down. Her breath caught in a hitch when his mouth found her, his sinful tongue darting inside of her. A delicious chill ran through her as he proceeded to devour her, a long-held sigh escaping her.

He continued to lick and suck her most sensitive spot, as if he were enjoying a meal. Her hands found their way into his hair, pressing him closer to her. She bucked and cried out, his hands wrapped around her thighs, holding her in place as she came.

She shuddered, and he lapped at her until she lay still, panting hard from her release.

He peered up at her, smiling. "Am I your first?"

She nodded slowly, not trusting her voice.

He moved back up and kissed her, letting her taste herself on his tongue. He pulled back and moved to nibble on her jaw. "This may hurt for a moment," he murmured near her ear.

"I trust you," she said, wrapping her arms around his neck.

His eyes met hers as he positioned the head of his cock, then slowly, he entered her.

She inhaled sharply, her back arching. He did not move, giving her time to adjust to the head of his prick before pushing in a little more. He grunted with every inch that went in until his entire length was inside her warmth.

"Are you all right?" he asked.

She bit her bottom lip lightly and nodded.

"I'm going to move now," he warned, watching her.

He moved his hips leisurely at first, each stroke long but gentle. She felt so full with him inside of her. His hips twisted as he pumped in and out of her, still slow and purposeful. He wanted her to feel good, and after a few moments, she did.

Her legs encircled his waist, her thighs squeezing him, urging him to move faster, to pump harder. He responded to her silent order, his pace increasing with greater force. He had been holding himself back for her sake.

She clawed at his back, hard enough to draw blood, but there was none. Her nails scraped across patches of scales, like armored plating down his spine. She could not hurt him. Ignoring the intrusive thoughts, she focused on the moment. A god had come from the heavens and was making love to her. He cared enough that he did not want to hurt her. Her orgasm built until she came undone, exploding beneath him.

"Zaven," she cried out, holding onto him tight.

He continued to move in and out of her until he had his own release.

Once she calmed, he gently brushed her sweat-soaked hair from her brow. His smile was warm despite how cold his body was. Considering how hot she was now, she welcomed it.

"How do you feel?" he asked.

She returned his smile. "Like I just made love to a god."

He chuckled at that, then gently pulled out of her, rolling onto his side.

She let out a sigh at the sensation. Though she did not say it aloud, she felt different. She turned on her side to face him, her hand lightly brushing his face.

"I didn't hurt you?"

"No," she murmured.

"Good," he smiled, his eyes hooded. He was falling asleep.

She grinned as his eyes shut, his arm draped possessively around her. Soon, she drifted off behind him.

CHAPTER 20

Restless beneath the silver glow of the moon, the celestial tides churned. Water lapped against the shore with a rhythm older than time, curling around the figures standing at the edge—three beings woven into the fabric of death itself, bound by duty.

Lux and Nox stood like guardians, Lux's tall frame towering over Nox, his long black hair in a loose braid over his shoulder, with a strip of white in the front. His skin was almost as dark as his hair, which made his golden eyes and perfect white teeth stand out more.

Nox was his opposite. She was small, dainty, with long white hair that had a strip of black in the front. She was pale as Zaven was, with an equally short temper and a foul mouth, but she was still nurturing as his mother should have been.

Zaven faced them, arms crossed, his dark hair stirring in the brine-heavy breeze. He had expected this conversation. He expected their worry after his confession about Airlia. Their judgment was anticipated, but he just did not care.

"She's mortal," Lux said, his voice carefully measured, like he was trying to keep this from turning into something worse.

"She won't live long," Nox added, softer, but not as certain.

Zaven cocked his head, observing them both with an expression that barely changed. "I know."

"And yet—" Lux narrowed his eyes, searching for something in his charge's stance. "You still refuse to let go."

Zaven sighed, shaking his head. "I refuse to pretend she doesn't matter."

Nox exchanged a glance with Lux before stepping closer, watching Zaven carefully. "She makes ya happy."

Zaven's lips curved, barely noticeable. "Yes."

Lux sighed, something troubled in his expression. "And when she's gone?"

Zaven did not flinch. His voice remained even. "Then I will mourn her."

"Yer playin' with time," Nox murmured.

Zaven's smirk deepened, something almost bitter threading into his voice. "Time plays with us all."

Lux exhaled suddenly, rubbing at his temple. "You have never been reckless before."

"Maybe I've grown tired of being careful."

The silence stretched between them.

Then Lux shook his head. "You are willing to suffer for this."

Zaven inhaled, the scent of the tide lingering, the salt mixing with the bitter taste of inevitability. "I think I already have."

Nox hesitated. "Then I hope yer ready for the cost."

Zaven did not answer. He did not need to.

CHAPTER 21

The sun had long since dipped below the horizon, leaving the sky painted in deep shades of blue and violet, the first stars flickering to life in the quiet expanse above. Airlia walked unhurriedly through the trees, the soft crunch of leaves beneath her feet the only sound breaking the stillness. There was something strange about the night—something gently pressing against her senses, coaxing her forward with quiet insistence.

Zaven had told her to meet him. He had not explained why, only that she would understand when she arrived.

She was not sure what she had expected. Their relationship had always carried an unspoken weight—something larger than words, larger than reason. There was the way he lingered near her now, the way his once gruff demeanor softened in the moments only they shared. She had learned how to read him in ways others could not—the quiet steadiness beneath his rough exterior, the way he listened even when he pretended not to care.

And now he was asking for her company. Here. At the river. The place where it had all begun.

The forest opened before her, the scent of water mingling with the crisp evening air. She hesitated at the edge of the clearing, her breath catching ever so slightly as she took in the sight before her.

The river was alive.

Not in the way it always was, flowing and endless—but in a way that felt deliberate, touched by something unseen. Lanterns flickered like stars brought down to earth, hanging from the branches, casting golden light across the water's surface. Soft petals floated along the current, carried gently downstream, their attendance delicate, thoughtful.

It was beautiful.

And in the center of it all—standing beneath the warm glow of the lanterns, dark hair catching in the night breeze—was Zaven.

Airlia's pulse thrummed.

Something about him was different that night. Not just his bearing, not just his usual steady observation—but the way he watched her. The way he was waiting.

She stepped forward.

And the moment stretched, silent and full.

Airlia swallowed, the realization setting in her bones. "Zaven…"

He stepped closer, his movements careful, deliberate, as if ensuring every second of the moment was counted, measured, remembered. "You once told me you were afraid of losing yourself," he murmured.

She gasped.

"I thought I understood that once," he continued, voice lower now, laced with something unspoken. "That being lost was inevitable. That loneliness wasn't something to fear—it was something to endure." He breathed out, shaking his head slightly, as if he were unlearning years of certainty. "And then you happened."

Airlia's chest tightened. "Zaven—"

"I want to be lost with you," he interrupted, voice steady but soft. "Not alone. Not wandering. But here."

She scarcely had time to think before he dropped to one knee. Her heartbeat stuttered.

Zaven reached into the folds of his cloak, pulling forth a ring carved from river stone, shaped by the waters that had nearly taken her—waters that had brought them together instead.

"I've never belonged to anything but the tide," he admitted. "But I belong with you. If you'll have me."

Airlia pressed a hand to her lips, emotions surging so fiercely she thought she might cry. And then—without hesitation, without doubt—she whispered, "Yes."

Zaven let out a slow lungful of air, something close to relief softening his features as he slid the ring onto her finger.

When he stood, she did not wait—she threw her arms around him, pulling him into a breathless, laughing embrace.

He brushed an errant tear from her cheek, a gentle smile on his face. He leaned forward and kissed her. When he pulled back, he held her gaze, leaning his forehead against hers. "Do you trust me?" he whispered.

She nodded, wondering what he was up to now, but she could see the lust in his eyes.

"Remove your dress," he ordered, a grin on his face.

"Here?" she asked, bewildered. "What if someone sees?"

"It'll be fine. I promise." He smiled reassuringly, then removed his cloak, followed by his tunic and trousers. "Would you like me to help you?"

She narrowed her eyes at him. "I can do it myself," she huffed.

He chuckled, watching her intently as she took off her dress and undergarments. Once she had neatly folded her clothes and set them aside, he held out his hand to her. She took it, and he led her to the river.

She hesitated.

"Don't worry, I won't let anything happen to you," he said, giving her hand a light squeeze.

"All right," she mumbled.

He stepped into the water, then helped her in. It was cold at first, but she quickly forgot about it when he kissed her again. He held her close as he walked backwards into a fallen tree that lay across the river. She was grateful they were in the shallow end of the water.

"I don't want you to fear the water anymore," he whispered into her lips. He turned so that she was against the tree, and before she could protest, his nimble fingers found her. She let out a gasp, his icy touch sending jolts of lightning through her.

"Ah, Zaven," she cried out.

He withdrew his fingers and turned her again so that the front of her was against the tree. With his knee, he spread her legs apart, his hand gliding over the expanse of her rear. He ran a finger up her slit, and she inhaled sharply.

"Zaven, please," she begged.

He chuckled at her plea, kissing her lovingly on the shoulder. He guided his cock to her entrance, rubbing the tip against her. A moan escaped her as she pushed back against him, urging him further inside of her. Despite how cold he and the water were, she felt hot all over, and when he plunged into her depths, she sighed with relief.

His strokes were long and slow at first. She moaned and cried out with every thrust. A surge of pure happiness washed over her as he sped up. But after a few moments, he pulled out. She whimpered at the sensation, feeling empty. He turned her back around to face him then. He had the devil in his eyes as he leaned her back and lifted her legs, spreading her for all to see. She rested her arms on the tree as he entered her again.

His thrusts were long again, drawn out, purposeful. She had never been so loved by a man before Zaven. Eldrin had cared for her, but she could never return his feelings. Especially not like this.

"Focus on me," he said in her ear, as if he could read her thoughts. "You are mine now, and I am yours. The water will never take you from me."

He pumped faster; she was close to climax. She shook Eldrin from her thoughts and focused on Zaven. With every moan and sigh, she drew even closer to her release. He dipped his head down and took one of her breasts into his mouth. His cool saliva did nothing to calm the heat that rose within her. The moment he bit down on her hardened nipple, she came screaming into the night. And with a grunt, he followed shortly after her.

The river flowed around them, quiet and endless. They both remained where they were, tired, but neither alone.

Her fear of the river was gone, replaced by a better memory.

CHAPTER 22

Zaven's private chambers were vast, carved from obsidian and veined with golden light. It was beautiful and comfortable, but that night it felt suffocating. Zaven had left Airlia to return to the celestial realm to say goodbye to his twin.

The air hummed with energy—unspoken, volatile—as he stood near the balcony, gazing down at the celestial sea below. His chambers were his sanctuary, once a place of contemplation and solitude. Now they were filled with the sound of his brother's rising fury.

Ozmir stood near the entrance to the balcony, blue eyes burning, hands clenched at his sides. He was trembling—not with fear, but with disbelief, with anger tangled in sorrow.

"You have gone too far," he said, his tone severe, accusing.

Zaven let out a breath—slow, measured—but did not turn. "Have I?" he asked dryly.

Ozmir stepped forward, voice tight with restrained emotion. "Don't mock me, Zaven. Mother will be cross with you for sneaking out once again."

"We're not children anymore, Ozzy. We can do as we please," he said absently, going back into his room.

"You reek of humans again," he hissed, following his twin. "You were with that human woman again, weren't you?"

Zaven said nothing. He did not need to.

Ozmir let out a shaky breath, as if saying the words aloud cemented the unbearable truth. "Mother won't like that you let her live."

"If she really cared, she would've found another way to kill her, but she hasn't," Zaven stated, his voice slightly edged with frustration. "She clearly doesn't care about one mortal or what we choose to do with them."

Ozmir leaned against the doorframe. "You know she's busy. She probably doesn't even know."

"And I suppose you'll tell her," he scoffed, rummaging through his things. He was not entirely sure what he was searching for, but he knew he would know it when he saw it.

"Not if you agree to stop seeing her and let her fate be what it may."

Zaven noted that his brother's anger was subsiding, but he knew the calm would not last. He still had not told him he was leaving and not coming back. "I can't agree to that," he said, still searching his room. "I feel different when I'm with her. I'm not a boring god, just a strange man that saved her life."

"Yes, twice now," Ozmir muttered, walking into the room.

It was three times, but Zaven did not feel the need to correct him.

"She really needs to stay away from water."

Zaven paused in his search briefly. "I love her, Ozzy," he sighed. "I think we were meant to be together."

Ozmir stared at him, stunned, then scented the air around his twin. "You've mated with a mortal! That's disgusting!"

Zaven growled, shoving his brother. "Shut your mouth."

Ever since their first argument, Zaven had noticed his brother's sudden disdain for mortals. They had switched sides.

"You're tainted," Ozmir roared, his anger rearing back up. "Mother will punish you severely for this."

Zaven's voice was steady, without remorse. "Who I lay with is no one's concern but my own. I'm going to be with her for as long as she lives, and no one will say otherwise."

Shaking his head, Ozmir spat, "Then there is no saving you."

Zaven could see that the words pained him to say, as if part of him had still clung to the hope that Zaven would take it all back, that he could undo what had been done. Zaven no longer cared.

He had found a glittering gold necklace with a sapphire pendant shaped like a wyvern, a small version of what he looked like in his bestial form. He wrapped the necklace around his wrist, then turned back to his brother. "Do what you must, little brother," Zaven sneered, forcing his way past his brother toward the balcony.

"Zaven! Zaven, where are you going?" Ozmir stumbled after his twin, his chest aching in a way he could not name.

The air split, energy crackling through the obsidian walls as Zaven dove off the balcony.

"Zaven? Zaven, please! I'm sorry. I won't say anything if you stay," Ozmir called out.

As he plummeted through the sky, the wind howled around him, tearing at his clothes as his human form shifted. Bones stretched and elongated, his fingers twisted into talons, his skin hardened into iridescent scales that shimmered in the fading sunlight. Wings erupted from his arms, connecting to his sides, unfurling wide, catching the air just before impact.

With a powerful beat, he propelled himself upward, his wyvern form surging toward the heavens. The clouds parted around him, mist curling against his newly formed snout as he released a roar. He could still hear his brother screaming his name.

Zaven turned his head to look at his brother's pleading face one last time. "Do what you want, Ozmir. I don't care anymore." With that, he flew off, leaving his twin to shout his name in vain.

CHAPTER 23

The forest was mostly still. High pines swayed gently overhead, their needles whispering to one another like watchers keeping counsel. The stream cut through the glade with quiet persistence, its surface reflecting the wan light of dusk. The wind stirred the tall grasses at the edge of the glade, brushing dark strands of Zaven's hair against his jaw as he moved along the riverbed. He had come alone, seeking a patch of hyssop for one of Airlia's remedies—simple, quiet work. Zaven stepped lightly over a fallen limb, intent on gathering hyssop near the water's edge when he felt it— wrongness. A pulse of intent.

He felt it before he saw him.

Eldrin emerged from the shadows beneath a leaning pine, his blade already drawn.

Zaven paused, his expression unreadable, gaze steady. "Bold," he said evenly.

Eldrin didn't respond. His eyes burned—not with fear, but with bitterness so deep it bordered on madness. "You should have left," he said.

Zaven's fingers curled subtly. "She made her choice."

"You took that choice from her," Eldrin snapped. "She couldn't see the spell you cast. But I see it."

Zaven stepped forward slowly, unarmed. "I cast nothing."

"You lie."

Eldrin surged forward, blade arcing toward Zaven's chest—fast, deliberate, deadly.

But Zaven was faster.

He spun aside; the blade whistling past his ribs, and retaliated with a palm to Eldrin's wrist. The sword jarred sideways, but didn't fall. Eldrin grunted, driving a shoulder into Zaven's midsection.

They crashed onto the damp earth.

Zaven shifted his weight mid-fall, rolled, and landed with a knee against Eldrin's chest. Eldrin kicked upward, throwing him off, both of them scrambling to their feet with the crunch of boots against stone and pine needles.

Eldrin slashed again—this time aiming for Zaven's throat—but Zaven ducked, caught Eldrin's arm, and twisted sharply. Bone strained. Eldrin snarled, head-butting Zaven to break the hold.

Zaven staggered back, but there was no blood drawn.

Eldrin lunged in the moment of weakness, blade raised for a final strike.

But Zaven stopped it.

With one sharp breath, he raised his hand and summoned water from the river behind him. It surged forward, coiling midair like a serpent, and slammed into Eldrin's chest, throwing him back against a birch trunk.

The sword flew from his grasp and skidded across the rocks.

When the fight ended, Eldrin collapsed to his knees, gasping, soaked, half-submerged in the stream's edge, arm twisted, lip bloodied, breath shallow.

Zaven strode forward, dripping water trailing behind him, gaze like frost under moonlight. He crouched beside Eldrin, grabbed his collar, and hauled him up just enough so their eyes met. "You wanted to kill me," Zaven said quietly.

Eldrin spat toward the ground, bitter. "You ruined her."

Zaven's jaw tightened—but his voice remained calm. "She saved me."

He let go, dropping Eldrin into the river's shallows.

"You deserve worse," Zaven said, standing over him. "But I won't give it to you."

Eldrin looked up, face pale with fury.

Zaven turned away. "Only because it would break her."

Eldrin lay frozen in the shallows, watching Zaven walk back into the trees—like mist reclaiming its shape.

The morning air was crisp, carrying the scent of fresh earth and the lingering sweetness of dried herbs from her cottage—their cottage. It had been weeks since Zaven had first moved in—weeks of quiet, of warmth, of something neither of them had quite named but had both embraced without hesitation.

It was different living together. Different in the way Airlia found his cloaks draped over her old wooden chair, or the way he had begun to quietly help with her healing work—not with mastery, but with care, handing her tools before she even had to ask. Different in the way she had grown accustomed to his presence, to his silence that was no longer detached but filled with understanding.

She had learned how he preferred his tea strong, how he would sit by the river at dusk, watching the water move as if listening to something only he could hear. She had learned that his grumpiness was mostly surface level, an armor against things he had never been given the chance to want. And now, for the first time, he wanted something more than solitude… her. And she wanted him.

It was why they were walking toward the village, steps slow but sure, fingers brushing but not fully intertwined.

They had decided together—spoken the words with quiet certainty beneath the lanterns by the river. Zaven had asked, not as a god, not as a creature lingering at the edges, but as someone who had found something worth staying for.

And Airlia had said yes.

Now, they were heading to the elder to ask for his blessing. It was mostly ceremonial—the village did not fully trust Zaven, would not entirely welcome him—but this was for her. For both of them.

Zaven had never asked to be accepted. He wanted only her.

The trees swayed gently as they stepped past the first cluster of homes, the smell of wood-smoke thick in the air. Villagers eyed them warily as they walked, whispers curling through the morning hush.

Airlia ignored them. Zaven did not flinch.

And then there was the ear-piercing, inhuman screech.

Airlia froze, gasping as the scent of burning suddenly thickened, acrid and unnatural. A scream split the air—a raw, terrified sound. The village was in chaos.

She turned just in time to see the creature descend. It had four black feathered wings and a bladed tail. She had seen nothing like it, but then she noticed its human-like appearance with its random patches of scales. It looked like Zaven.

Fire shot out from its hands, its movements reckless, tearing through carts, through homes, sending villagers running in all directions as it picked some of them off, one by one.

And then—too quickly—the villagers turned to Zaven.

"You brought this!" someone shouted.

"This is his doing!" another cried.

The accusations slammed into the air like arrows.

Zaven's jaw clenched, but he did not respond.

Airlia pushed forward, her heart pounding, stepping between Zaven and the furious crowd. "Stop this! He didn't bring it here!"

The villagers did not listen.

"Then why does it look like him?" someone asked.

A tremor split the ground as the beast's tail lashed once more, shattering a wooden cart, sending splinters flying. The beast's movements were unhinged, its rage unrelenting, nothing but death and destruction in its wake.

Zaven's expression darkened, his eyes locking onto the beast. "This ends now," he growled.

Airlia saw it then—the way he stiffened, the way his presence shifted, growing heavier, stronger. "What are you going to do?" she asked, voice hushed but steady.

Zaven did not answer. Instead, he stepped forward—toward the beast, toward the chaos, toward the thing that had turned a fearful village against him.

He was no longer just the man she loved. He was a god. And the battle was his.

The ground trembled beneath the force of the creature's fury, its wings slicing through the air, sending gales rippling across the burning village. Flames licked at the rooftops, thick smoke curling into the sky as its bladed tail crashed into the earth, carving deep scars into the soil.

The villagers continued shouting accusations—fear twisting their voices into something ugly—but he ignored them. He had no time for their ignorance, nor patience for their misplaced anger.

He exhaled slowly. Then he moved.

Water surged beneath his feet, rippling outward as it responded to his command. The well behind him answered first—its surface churning violently before rising in intense, coiling tendrils, twisting like serpents. The beast's eyes moved toward Zaven—recognizing, sensing, knowing. It lunged.

Zaven did not move.

The moment the creature struck, Zaven turned the water against it. The water twisted, lashing out in controlled torrents, slamming into the beast's wings, forcing it to stagger mid-flight. It roared, thrashing against the liquid restraints, trying to shake free.

But Zaven was not done. His fingers curled slightly, scarcely perceptible—but it was enough. The blood within the beast's body slowed, thickening under his influence, turning sluggish, resisting its body's commands. The creature faltered, its movements becoming heavy, weighted. It roared in frustration, fighting against forces it had never known before.

Zaven's countenance did not change. With a final, hard pull, he forced the blood in the creature's veins to halt for a fraction of a second—just enough.

The beast crumpled, wings wavering, its tail just missing the ground as its body convulsed, trying to override the unnatural stillness.

Zaven stepped forward, his presence sharp as steel. He did not need to raise his voice. "Enough."

The word rippled through the air—not a shout, not a command. A decree. The water tightened, dragging the creature to him, forcing submission. And then—finally—after one last desperate thrash, the beast stilled. Flames appeared, licking at its body, consuming the creature whole, leaving behind an ashen husk in the twisted form of the beast. As the wind blew, the husk broke down; the ashes scattered on the breeze.

Silence fell over the village.

Zaven exhaled, rolling his shoulders, his gaze still steady, still cold. He turned.

And the villagers, once so eager to blame him, now stood in stunned, uneasy awe.

Airlia rushed to his side, embracing him. "What was that creature?"

"An Andr," he replied, voice even. "They are normally immortal and will regenerate after death, but that one won't."

She furrowed her brow. "Why not?"

"Because I was the one that killed it," he said flatly.

She saw the pained look in his eyes but said nothing more.

CHAPTER 24

The village still hummed with unease.

Though Zaven had saved them, had killed the Andr before it could do even more harm, the people remained wary. Their gratitude was reluctant, spoken in hushed tones, given without warmth. The way their eyes lingered on him was unchanged—uncertain, mistrustful, afraid. His brutal slaying of the Andr left them deeply worried. He could manipulate blood, and that was a dangerous power.

But Airlia stood beside him, and that was enough.

They had just stepped past the healer's hut when an angry, familiar voice cut through the air.

"You."

Zaven did not react immediately. But Airlia stiffened, turning just as Eldrin strode forward, his appearance tight with something indecipherable—something caught between frustration and loss. He had been away for some time, visiting his sister in another village. She had hoped the distance would dull his anger, that perhaps the time apart would soften his resentment.

It had not.

Eldrin's gaze darted between them, his posture tense. "You're still here," he muttered, eyes narrowing on Zaven.

Zaven breathed out quietly, his look dry. "Obviously."

The air between them was taut, heavy with something unspoken but undeniable.

Eldrin stood rigid, jaw set tight with irritation barely contained. His aura carried the weight of things left unsaid for too long, and now, standing before them, he had no intention of holding them back.

"You never told me what he is," Eldrin said, his voice low, cutting through the stillness like a blade.

Airlia let out a mouthful of air, tired but patient. "I told you before, Eldrin. It's not your concern."

He huffed, shaking his head. "Not my concern?" He turned his glare back to Zaven, his expression darkening. "Everyone in this village fears him. No one knows what he is, why he's here, or what he's doing. And you expect me to just accept that?"

Zaven, as always, remained composed, unreadable. His dark hair caught the soft glow of the morning light; his demeanor unwavering under Eldrin's scrutiny. "I don't expect anything from you," he said, voice calm, almost indifferent.

Eldrin's lip curled faintly, irritation creeping into his stance. "You think that makes it better? That you can just linger here, living among us, living with her—" His fingers twitched at his sides, like he was fighting the urge to say something he knew he would regret. "You've bewitched her."

Airlia narrowed her eyes. "Don't," she warned.

Eldrin huffed a humorless laugh, looking between them. "You won't even deny it."

Zaven raised an unimpressed brow. "Would it matter if I did?"

Eldrin's teeth clenched. "You're hiding something."

Airlia took a step forward, voice steady. "What if we are? And if I knew exactly what he was? Would it change anything?"

Eldrin gasped slightly, barely perceptible. He had expected pushback—had expected denial, maybe even guilt. But there were none. There was only conviction. And that made something inside him tighten painfully. She could see it all.

"You're throwing away everything for him," he muttered, voice quieter now, edged with something raw, something bruised.

Airlia swallowed, but her expression did not waver. "I'm choosing him."

The words landed heavier than she meant them to.

Eldrin's nostrils flared. He let out a short, sharp bit of air, rubbing a hand over his face like he was trying to suppress whatever was unraveling inside him.

Then he spoke.

"I saw you two that night—in the river under the lanterns," he started.

Airlia flushed red immediately, but Zaven's look remained the same.

"You thought you were alone, but I was there watching."

Then Zaven grinned. "Did you enjoy yourself?"

Eldrin's rage flared. "How could you let him touch you like that?" he roared.

"Keep your voice down," Airlia fussed quietly.

"What would your father think?" he growled low, demanding.

Airlia's face scrunched up in anger. "He would think so long as I'm happy that it's fine," she countered.

"He won't even defend your honor," Eldrin spat, gesturing to Zaven.

"Because I don't need to," Zaven replied.

Eldrin's mouth pressed into a thin line, frustration crackling in the space between them. His throat worked as if he were struggling to get the words out. And then they finally came. "I'm leaving."

Airlia blinked wildly in shock, but only for a moment.

"So long as you're with him," he continued, voice tight, "I have no place here."

Silence settled between them.

Airlia absorbed his words, weighed them carefully. And then, softly, she nodded. "I understand."

Eldrin's eyes snapped to hers, searching—hoping, perhaps, for something else. But there was nothing.

She offered him a small, polite smile. "I wish you well."

The finality of it lingered.

His throat worked again, more frustration mounting, his eyes darting to Zaven as if hoping for something different there, too. But Zaven only watched him quietly, knowingly.

Eldrin swore under his breath. "Fine," he muttered. "Do what you want."

Then, without another word, he turned on his heel and stormed off.

Airlia breathed out slowly, watching him go.

Zaven glanced at her. "You expected that."

She nodded. "I did."

"Are you sad?"

She rolled her shoulders before tilting her head toward him. "Did you really bewitch me?" she asked, grinning.

He frowned. "You know that I didn't."

"Did you know he was there that night? Watching us?"

He nodded. "I did."

She furrowed her brow. "Why didn't you say anything?"

"Would it have mattered?"

She thought about it for a long moment. Then she shook her head. "No."

Zaven did not reply. Instead, he simply reached for her hand, threading his fingers through hers.

And Airlia squeezed back.

He glanced at her, studying her face carefully. "Then let's finish what we came here for."

The village elder sat outside his home, his look wise but weary. He had seen much over the years—too much to be surprised, too much to fear things he did not understand.

Airlia and Zaven stood before him, quiet but sure.

"You wish to marry," the elder said simply.

"Yes," Airlia answered.

The elder's gaze shifted to Zaven, lingering for a moment. "You know they will never accept you."

"I don't need their acceptance." His voice was calm, certain. "Only hers."

Airlia smiled softly.

The elder breathed out casually, considering them both.

Then, after a long pause, he nodded. "Then I give you my blessing."

And just like that, it was done. But they would tell no one.

CHAPTER 25

The fields were dying.

Airlia knelt in the brittle stalks of wheat, running her fingers across the dry earth, feeling how lifeless it had become. Four years had passed since Zaven had come into her life. Since he had pulled her from the river, since he had stepped past every wall she had built, since she had chosen him. In that time, they had learned the quiet routines of each other's existence, the way their lives wove together effortlessly.

When he was not off guiding drowned souls, she had taught him how to recognize the scent of herbs before plucking them. He had learned to anticipate her needs before she voiced them. He had become a presence she could lean into—not hovering, not suffocating, but steady. They had built something her father would be proud of.

And yet—this.

The village had suffered poor harvests before, but never like this. The air was dry, heavy with the scent of decay. First, the animals grew weaker, their bodies becoming frail, their movements slow. Then the land followed. Cracks splitting across the fields, the crops withering before they could be harvested.

And with the dying earth came the whispers.

Airlia heard them in passing, in hushed conversations outside the healer's hut, in the wary glances thrown in her direction.

"This started after he came."

"He's not meant to be here. It's unnatural."

"The land rejects him."

"She summoned a demon. She must be a witch."

Airlia pressed her lips together, trying to keep the biting sting of frustration from settling too deep. This was her village. These were her people. How could they think so low of her when they watched her grow up?

They were always searching for someone or something to blame. And, as always, they had turned to Zaven. She found him by the river, as she always did, kneeling beside the water, hands damp with soil from the roots he had just unearthed. He had taken to helping with her healing work in ways no one else had ever offered. Preparing salves, gathering herbs, taking quiet, unseen burdens so she would not have to bear them alone.

He had grown accustomed to this. To quiet work, to sharing his existence with hers. But even as she stepped closer, she saw it—the tension in his shoulders, the way his fingers tightened slightly against the dirt.

"They blame me," he said, his voice low.

Airlia sighed, kneeling beside him, dusting off her palms. "Of course they do."

Zaven snorted, staring into the water. "It's foolish."

"It is." She tilted her head slightly, watching him. "But that won't stop them."

He was quiet for a long moment, fingers tracing the edges of the yarrow sprig without thought. Then he said, "You want me to leave."

Airlia swallowed, shaking her head. "No. I would never ask that of you. I know what it means for you to be here with me."

"But?"

She hesitated. "I think… it would be safer if you stayed clear of the village for now."

Zaven did not react immediately. He only stared at the river, watching the current shift. Then, after a long, stretched silence, he nodded. "I'll stay away."

Her throat tightened, but she knew it was the right choice.

Still, the thought of seeing him less, of keeping him away because of fear rooted in ignorance—it made her feel raw, unsettled. Especially when he was doing so much good. But she had heard how witch hunts went, and she did not want to give them any reason to hurt him.

She reached for his hand, curling her fingers around his. "This won't last forever," she promised.

Zaven's gaze flashed toward her, studying her face, her certainty. "I don't believe in forever," he mumbled, but he squeezed her hand back.

CHAPTER 26

The air was heavy with the scent of drying earth; the sun casting long golden streaks across the dying fields. The village sat just beyond the thinning treeline, quiet in a way that spoke of unrest rather than peace.

Zaven had not meant to wander so close.

Most days, he avoided it, as Airlia had asked him to. He stayed near the river, away from prying eyes, away from the whispers. He had spent the last four years easing himself into the fragile edges of her world—helping her tend to the sick, learning the subtle ways in which life flourished outside of death's grasp.

The land had not rejected him. But the villagers believed otherwise. Their crops were failing, their livestock weakening, and they had turned their blame toward the thing they feared most. Him.

He had learned to endure their resentment, had heard it in passing before, spoken in hushed tones, carried by the wind when they believed him too far to hear.

Today, however, their voices carried loudly. Angry. And he was close enough to hear every word.

"I knew this would happen," one of them muttered. "A demon who doesn't belong among humans has no place in our village."

"This sickness started after she brought him here," another said, accusatory, more vicious.

Airlia. They were talking about Airlia. His chest tightened.

"He was never meant to be here," a third voice interjected. "She should have left him to whatever darkness he came from. Now look at us."

A scoff followed, rough and bitter. "Perhaps she's cursed now, too."

Zaven did not move. He did not react—not outwardly—but something inside him had shifted. The ground beneath his feet felt different now, less steady, less solid, as though reality had become malleable in the hands of his anger.

They did not know him. They did not know what had truly brought the rot to their fields. Neither did he. Despite that, they blamed him. Blamed her.

Another voice broke the murmurs, a low tone, softer, but no less cruel. "She could have chosen any man. A hunter, like Eldrin. But she chose that."

A harsh laugh. "Can you imagine what their children would look like? She has damned herself with him."

Zaven exhaled slowly, his breathing controlled, measured—too much so. The air around him shifted, and the creek behind him curled in reaction to his restraint. He had heard enough.

Without a word, he turned on his heel. And this time, when he walked, he did not linger.

Cloaked in his magic, he walked through the village unseen. He worried for Airlia, and though he had agreed to stay away, he needed to check on her. For her and him.

The air inside the healing hut was thick with the scent of dried herbs, smoke curling faintly from burning sprigs of juniper Airlia had placed in a clay bowl near the door. The room was dimly lit, the late afternoon light filtering through the woven slats of the window, casting golden streaks against the wooden floor.

Zaven lingered at the entrance, watching her in silence.

The old woman sat in her usual place, her thin hands resting on her lap, her bones fragile beneath the weight of years. Airlia sat beside the old woman, carefully smoothing salve over the gnarled skin of her hands. Her touch was gentle, precise, but there was something heavier in her posture—something absent in the way her shoulders had always carried their quiet strength.

She looked tired. Sad.

The old woman blew air out sharply through her nose, shifting against the blankets draped over her thin form. "A shame," she muttered, her voice rough, edged. "You were such a promising girl."

Airlia did not lift her head, her hands steady as she continued tending to the woman's aching joints. "I still am," she said softly.

The old woman scoffed, shaking her head. "Not anymore." Her eyes flickered toward the open door, toward nothing, toward something unseen. "Not since you gave yourself to that demon."

Zaven's expression did not change. He was used to being called a demon.

Airlia swallowed but kept her movements controlled, refusing to let the sting of the words sink in too deeply. "He is my husband."

"He is cursed."

Zaven shifted behind Airlia. He could tell she sensed him—like a breath in the space between moments, like a ripple of water against the shore.

Airlia inhaled slowly, pressing her lips together, letting the air out through her nose. "You don't know him."

The old woman shifted, her bony fingers curling in her lap. "I don't need to."

The silence that followed was thick, weighted. And then something changed. The air pulsed, subtle but undeniable. He knew Airlia felt it—his anger. A warmth curled against her skin, featherlight but firm, settling across her shoulders like a presence wrapping itself around her.

She closed her eyes and whispered his name.

Exhaling softly, she brushed the last strip of cloth around the woman's wrist, securing it gently. "I will bring you more balm tomorrow."

Then, without another word, she stood to leave. And Zaven followed.

CHAPTER 27

He made it home long before she did. He had no longer wanted to hear the awful things being said about his wife, and he did not want her to know he was there. Though he was sure she likely knew. She always had a way of feeling him before seeing him.

The sun had begun to set by the time she made it home. He heard the heavy sigh she let out before she pushed the door to their cottage open. They wed in secret, yet she claimed him as her husband to the old woman she was helping. It pleased him greatly—more than he thought it would have—and he greeted her as he always did. With love and excitement. The state of her stamped his enthusiasm out.

"My ethereal one, what happened to you?" Gently, he peeled a piece of rotten fruit from her hair.

More rotted food stained her dress, and she was damp and sticky.

"It is nothing, my love. I am fine," she lied, as she forced a smile, fighting back unshed tears.

The villagers were small-minded, saying such awful things about her when they thought she was not within earshot, or maybe they wanted her to know how they felt. How they blamed them for all that was going wrong. How they thought she was mad for being with a demon rather than a more suitable man from the village. They could only imagine what their children would look like. But they would never have any. He was not a living man and could not produce children. Airlia said she was fine with it, but he knew better.

He wanted to kill them all for bringing it up where she could hear them, but he did not for her sake. They already thought he was a monster. There was no need to prove it. So, he embraced his wife, but did not push her to talk about it. "Then sit and rest," he said, smiling warmly.

She took the seat that was offered, returning his smile. "Tell me of your day? I know it gets lonely for you having to stay inside while I'm away."

He shook his head, fetching a wet cloth to clean her with. "It's fine, my love," he lied. "I don't mind it at all." It ate him up inside, having to be away from her, leaving her to be pelted with old, rotten food.

"If my people weren't so fearful of strangers that look—" She stopped what she was saying when the realization of her words hit.

So, he finished for her. "That look like me," he said, his face somber.

She scrubbed her face before handing him the rag. "I love the way you look," she said, a genuine smile on her face.

He knelt in front of her, and she gently cupped his face. "I think your scales are beautiful."

She stroked the scales at his hairline, behind his ears. Enjoying her warmth, he closed his eyes.

When she leaned forward and kissed him ardently, she whispered, "Make love to me," against his lips.

As he lifted her from the chair, his lips captured hers. He was more than happy to oblige her request, and he carried her to their bedroom. He gently set her back on her feet, and they both removed their clothes. A few moments passed as they took the time to admire each other in the nude. Her skin was the color of fresh cream against the fiery red of her long hair. She had full, pale-pink lips and crystal-blue eyes. It finally hit him that she did not look like anyone else in the village. She stood out as much as he did. It was only natural that they fell in love with each other. She was beautiful and perfect.

Closing the small distance between them, he kissed her again. Gently, he picked her back up and placed her on the bed. After carefully mounting her, he stared lovingly at her and whispered, "I love you so much."

She stroked the scales at the nape of his neck, something he enjoyed, and smiled adoringly up at him.

He entered her little by little, reveling in the warmth around him. His pace was steady, purposeful, as he watched how her face flushed with pure ecstasy. He shut his eyes, wanting to focus on each cry and moan he coaxed out of her, her breathing labored. It did not take long before she climaxed, calling out his name as she shuddered beneath him. He smiled. She really did give herself to him.

"What has you so pleased?" she asked between breaths.

"You," he grinned, dipping his head to lightly nip one of her breasts. Her nipples were the perfect shade of pale pink.

She hissed, arching into him as he sucked the taut nipple into his mouth.

"You'll pay for that," she growled playfully, pushing him off of her and onto his back.

She straddled his waist backwards, and he enjoyed the sight of her wide rear within his view.

"What are you up to?" he asked, brow furrowed. He grunted, then hissed when she touched him.

She peered over her shoulder at him, the devil in her sly smile. "Your cock is still hard. You haven't had your release yet."

"And what do you intend to do about it?" he was genuinely curious. She had never been so bold before.

"I intend to please my husband properly," she grinned.

The heat of her womanhood was close to his aching erection, and she was still soaked from her release. First, she took hold of him, her small, calloused hand rough against the sensitive skin of his cock. Again, he hissed at the sensation. Then she rubbed her wet slit against him, moaning as she rocked back and forth. His idle hands found their way to her rear, lightly massaging the soft flesh before kneading it.

Zaven watched as his wife continued to rub herself against him as she stroked him, her free hand going to her breast and twisting the nipple. She threw her head back as her hips moved faster and pressed harder against him until she came again. When she calmed, she peered at him over her shoulder, a pout on her perfect lips.

"Are you not satisfied?" she asked, concern in her tone, edged with frustration.

"Almost," he chuckled. "You're welcome to continue. I'm enjoying myself."

She growled, facing forward. Raising her hips, she guided him into her, sinking down as she engulfed every inch of him in the warmth of her core. She let out a contented sigh once she had all of him inside of her again. Her hands found their way to her breasts, massaging them as she rotated her hips.

Airlia was pleasuring herself on top of him, and he could not help but enjoy it. It was so erotic and out of character for her.

He grabbed her by the hips, slowing her pace as she ground herself into him. He wanted her to last a little longer this time, but he was getting close after all her hard work.

With another grunt, he erupted beneath her, and she followed behind him. She slumped forward, her breath ragged.

"At last," she gasped, rolling off of him.

He laughed tiredly, pulling her close when she crawled up beside him. He pulled the fur blanket over them when he felt her shiver. His body provided no warmth for her, but still she cuddled up to him. Soon, she had drifted off to sleep. She was well and truly spent. He eventually followed her into slumber, hoping tomorrow would be better for them both.

CHAPTER 28

Curling over the river's surface, the mist twisted in slow, deliberate motions, as if reluctant to surrender the soul beneath its depths.

Zaven stood at the edge, his presence a shadow against the shifting fog. He had felt the call long before he arrived—the faint tug at the edges of his awareness, the undeniable pull toward the water's grasp.

Another drowned soul. Another lingering spirit refusing to cross.

Lux appeared beside him, his dark robes rippling in the unseen current, his face calm but expectant. "You took your time."

Zaven exhaled intensely, his gaze fixed on the rippling water. "I have other obligations."

Lux tilted his head. "A mortal life doesn't outweigh death."

Zaven did not answer. He hated leaving Airlia after the night they had. He hated leaving her, period, but he had his duties. She understood.

Zaven stepped forward, lifting a hand, fingers curling toward the surface. The river shuddered, answering him instantly, parting just enough to reveal the figure beneath—the man who had fought against fate longer than most. A stubborn old man from the village.

He recognized him immediately. The wrinkled lines of his face, the deep grooves of time etched into his skin. He had seen him before—in passing, lingering at the edges of the healer's hut, muttering about Airlia's choices, about the man she had chosen.

Now he was here. Dead. Waiting. And still unwilling.

The old man scowled, looking between them with hard, glaring eyes. "I'm not ready."

Lux sighed, rubbing his temples in slow frustration. "They never are, the elderly."

Zaven rolled his shoulders, his expression one of irritation. "You don't have a choice."

The old man's lip curled. "I do. I won't go."

Lux muttered something to himself before giving Zaven a pointed look. "Handle this."

Zaven exhaled, stepping closer, letting his authority weigh into the space between them. "You will cross," he said simply, his voice devoid of argument.

The river groaned—felt his will.

The old man stiffened. "I knew you was a demon."

For a long, tense moment, neither moved. Then—slowly, inevitably—Zaven lifted his hand once more, and the river *dragged* the soul downward, swallowing it whole.

The mist settled.

Lux hummed, watching the ripples fade. "You're more efficient when you're impatient."

Zaven gave him a stern look. "You interrupted my morning."

Lux smirked. "Don't let your mortal distract you too much."

Zaven did not respond. Instead, he turned, and he left.

The sun hung low by the time Zaven stepped through the threshold of their home, the scent of dried herbs lingering in the air, familiar but faint.

He expected to hear her humming—soft, absentminded—as she worked through her remedies. He expected to see the water boiling for tea, the faint outline of her figure moving between the shelves, gathering supplies.

But the cottage was still. Empty.

He frowned, glancing toward the door, scanning the space for signs of recent movement. Nothing. She was not there.

It was not unusual. Airlia spent hours tending to the village, gathering herbs, treating wounds, exhausting herself for people who refused to see her worth.

Still, something in his chest tightened.

He shook off the unease, stepping toward the fireplace, letting himself sink into the chair he had claimed as his own.

He would wait. She would return.

CHAPTER 29

The air in the village square was thick—dense with judgment, with fear, with something far darker.

Airlia stood before them, wrists bound, her breathing steady despite the weight pressing against her chest. The crowd gathered in tight clusters, their eyes sharp, their whispers crawling through the space like insects. The accusations had spread like wildfire—words spoken in fear twisting into something irreversible.

"Witch!"

"Consorting with a demon!"

"Cursed!"

She had known their hatred for Zaven ran deep, but she had not expected this—to be dragged from their home, to be thrown before the new elder and made to stand trial like some forsaken thing.

And now—now he was here. Eldrin.

He stood tall among them, his bearing carrying a twisted sense of triumph, though his face remained carefully schooled. His testimony had sealed her fate.

"She bewitched me! Made me love her until she was done with me," he said, voice steady, unwavering. "I saw her give herself to the demon many times. In the river, like a ritual. She pledged herself to him."

A murmur rippled through the crowd. About the tainted water supply for crops and animals.

Airlia inhaled intensely, searching him, studying every inch of his face. Something was not right. Something was not Eldrin.

"Look, she even wears his talisman around her neck." He pointed to the wyvern pendant Zaven had given her years ago.

His eyes were wrong. His voice was too precise.

"She used her demon to heal my wounds," one person shouted from the crowd. "I'm cursed now."

"I saw him command the water," another proclaimed.

The elder shifted in his seat, leaning forward. "The evidence is clear," he declared. "She is guilty. She will be executed at dusk."

The crowd erupted. Some in approval, some merely watching with cautious unease.

Airlia barely heard them. Her attention remained on Eldrin. Or whatever stood in his place.

The damp stone walls pressed against the silence, heavy with the weight of inevitability.

Airlia sat on the narrow cot, wrists still bound, breathing evenly despite the storm raging beneath her skin.

The door creaked open. In stepped Eldrin.

She did not flinch, did not react—only watched him carefully as he moved through the dim light, his movements too smooth, too calculated.

"You lied to them," she said simply.

He smirked. "Did I?"

Airlia let out air slowly, tilting her head ever so slightly. "You're not Eldrin."

The figure before her chuckled, shaking his head as if amused. "No," he admitted. "I'm not."

She swallowed, waiting.

And then, with a slow, deliberate movement, his form melted. The illusion faded, unraveling like mist in the cold. And there—standing before her in his true form— was Zaven. But it was not him.

Her breath caught.

His golden hair gleamed in the dim light, his blue eyes holding none of Zaven's warmth, none of his quiet patience. His scales were a cold, pristine white lined in gold.

"You will die for what you've taken from me," he grumbled, his voice smooth, edged with something final.

Airlia inhaled sharply, straightening her posture. "I have taken nothing."

His countenance darkened. "You took him."

Her pulse thudded.

"You made him stay." His face tightened. "You made him forget what he is."

She held his gaze, refusing to turn away. "He didn't forget."

He scoffed, stepping closer, tilting his head slightly. "You think I'll let this stand? That I'll let you tear him from his purpose? From me?"

Airlia swallowed but did not answer.

He smiled faintly, something cold, cruel. "At dusk, it won't matter."

The weight of his words settled. Then—without another word—he turned. And he left her in the dark.

CHAPTER 30

In the hearth, the fire had burned low, casting soft shadows against the stone walls of their cottage. The scent of juniper lingered faintly in the air, clinging to the wooden beams, to the woven blankets, to everything that still carried the scent of her.

But she was not there.

She should have returned by now.

Zaven stood motionless, staring at the empty space before him, feeling something heavy settle deep in his ribs—a quiet warning, an ache that had no name. The air felt different. Even the river had grown restless.

Something was wrong.

His breath came sharp, measured, too controlled as he stepped toward the door, pushing it open, letting the cool evening wind rush past his skin.

Then he was moving.

The village square was alive with chaos.

Shouts cracked through the air, fists curled around jagged stones, fear turning into blind hatred as they cast their judgement without hesitation.

Airlia.

She knelt in the center, barely upright, her body shaking under the weight of the blows that had already landed. Blood trickled down from her temple, ran slick down her arms, smeared against the dirt beneath her knees. Her breathing was harsh, uneven—fighting against the pain, fighting against the inevitability curling at the edges of her vision. But she did not cry out. She was still fighting.

Zaven did not move. He did not breathe. He simply watched. Watched as they shattered her, piece by piece. Watched as she finally fell.

Something inside him cracked open, too wide, too deep. The ground beneath him pulsed, the creek behind him shuddering in reaction to his rage, to his grief, to the unnatural stillness that had rotted itself in his limbs.

It took everything in him to step forward. To reach her.

The moment he stepped into the clearing, the villagers stiffened, some drawing back instinctively, as if sensing the shift in the air before truly seeing him. He did not speak. Did not waste time on empty words.

He reached her. Dropped to his knees. Gathered her into his arms.

She was shaking. Cold. Dying.

He pressed his forehead against hers, breath uneven. "My ethereal one."

She gasped softly, her fingers twitching against his tunic, but her strength was failing her. "Zaven—"

"Stay still." His voice was low, firm, edged with something raw.

She swallowed, breath unsteady, her body curling against his chest. "It hurts."

He clenched his jaw, his grip tightening. "I can fix this."

Her brow furrowed weakly, eyes fluttering open just enough to meet his. "No."

His expression darkened, something strong flashing behind his eyes. "Airlia—"

"There is an order to things, remember?" she interrupted. Her voice was quieter now, rasping yet steady, still certain. "I have escaped death too many times."

"You can do it again," his voice cracked, chest tightening.

Her lips parted, shaking faintly—before pressing into the smallest, most fragile smile. "Not this time."

Zaven exhaled angrily, desperation curling at the edges of his composure. "I can take it from you—the pain. I can pull the blood back into place, I can—"

"No," her fingers weakly pressed against his wrist, her touch barely there, barely clinging. "You can't."

He swallowed hard, his grip firm but gentle, his body stilling.

Airlia's lips trembled, her breath coming in slow, shallow fragments. "Promise me."

His jaw tightened. "I—" He stopped himself, taking in air deeply, forcing his rage to settle. Then softer, quieter. "I promise."

The relief washed over her almost instantly, her body sinking further into his arms, her fingers curling just slightly against his sleeve.

"I will make them pay," he growled, glaring at the stunned crowd.

"No." She swallowed, voice breaking, raw. "Not them."
He stiffened.

Her bloody fingers pressed against his chest. A silent plea. "Don't hurt them. It's not their fault."

His throat tightened. He wanted to refuse. He wanted to punish them, to tear them apart. But her gaze, weak and failing, held him still.

"You have to promise," she whispered.

He clenched his jaw, drawing in a sharp, controlled breath. "I promise."

Her body relaxed again, ever so slightly—her lips parting, breath shallow, uneven. She tried to speak. Tried to tell him something. But her voice never came. She exhaled once. And then—nothing. Silence. A void, endless and cruel.

Zaven pressed her closer against him, refusing to let go.

The creek behind them trembled. And the village held its breath.

EPILOGUE

Calmly, gently, he laid her body down. He stood, his body shaking ever so slightly. His head held down, staring at his beloved. Since she had not drowned, he could not see her soul off to the afterlife. But he knew his sister would care for her. He felt when her soul departed; she had accepted her fate and was ready to move on. Ready to leave him.

Once he felt her leave, his eyes snapped to the hushed crowd in front of him. His rage was a tangible thing, a living beast inside him. And none of them showed any remorse for what they had just done. They had taken her from him. And he was not ready to let her go.

His fingers flexed at his sides as he glared at them. Some backed away, feeling the change in the air. The small creek rumbled, and the well shuddered as the water began to boil and evaporate. Then, the plants began to wither and die. A sound, a sizzle, followed by a pop in the air. The air was suddenly dry, and it was far too hot. His rage swelled.

Then they all screamed. They ran in all directions. But it did not matter to him. The sky darkened. His fury could not be contained. Would not be stopped.

"Please!" someone shouted.

"Spare us!" came another.

Each one popped like a fluid-filled sack, blood splattering all over the dry, cracked earth. Every man, every woman, and every child near him exploded in quick succession, their blood and organs hitting the next person before they too erupted in a spray of entrails. There would be no survivors. Though she had made him promise with her dying breath, he could not keep it. Their senseless prejudice led to her death. He could not let them live.

Those that did not explode died choking on their own blood as it boiled in their bodies, melting their skin. He was upsetting the natural order, and he knew it was wrong, but he was grieving, and he did not care. The soul of the one he loved—an innocent—had gone too soon. He would accept whatever punishment his fellow gods saw fit to give him.

Soon, there was no one left to kill. All that remained were blood-boiled bodies, some with the bones of others sticking out of them. Not even the animals survived his wrath.

He dropped to his knees, exhausted, tears running down his face. Turning his head up to the heavens, he howled in anguish into the night. He could no longer fathom life— or immortality—without her. Before he collapsed, Lux and Nox appeared at his side. As the darkness engulfed him, he prayed he would wake up and this would all just be a bad dream.

OTHER WORKS BY
EMBER DRAKE

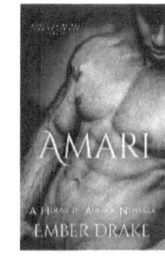

About the Author

Ember Drake is an American author from Columbia, South Carolina. She has been writing since the age of ten and has aspired to be a published author ever since. Ember has always had a love of dragons and wolves. As a joke, she was told that all she needed was to put them together and then she would be happy. This resulted in the creation of Raesh, who was modeled after her favorite former Power Ranger, Johnny Yong Bosch. Roland/Zaven was modeled after her favorite actor, Matt Ryan.

She had been working on the House of Ausher series since the age of seventeen. It was just three short stories that only included vampires and werewolves, both of which she is a huge fan of. The series evolved from terrible Backstreet Boys fan fiction about three brothers to what it is today.

Visit EmberDrakeAuthor.com for news and updates!

www.ingramcontent.com/pod-product-compliance
Lightning Source LLC
Chambersburg PA
CBHW050900180626
46814CB00007B/2814